WHITE NOISE

UNEXPECTED BOOK TWO

ANN GRECH

ISBN: 978-0-9954321-4-7

Ann Grech may be contacted via the following email address:

ann@anngrech.com

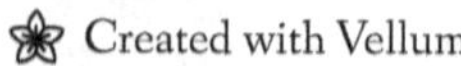 Created with Vellum

Bisexual sports star, Reef Reid, is back in action on the slopes with his new boyfriend, paramedic, Ford Wallace by his side. Taking the next step in their relationship was supposed to be easy, but fate has other plans. Will they be able to hold out against the forces trying to tear them apart?

Paramedic and mountain rescuer, Stratford 'Ford' Wallace, fell hard and fast for pro-snowboarder, Reef Reid. For a 'straight' guy, falling in love with a dude was unexpected, but his attraction to Reef is undeniable. Neither of them have uttered those three little words yet, but Ford knows Reef feels the same. At least, he thinks he does.

Reef is smashing his pre-season training at Fernie, the idyllic Canadian snow resort, getting wicked air and landing what could be season-winning jumps. What's even better is that his man is with him. Going home to Ford every night is what Reef always dreamed of—his very own happily ever after.

Knowing they're ready, they take the next step in their relationship—meeting the parents. But when tragedy strikes on the slopes, can Ford push through the painful memories and be what Reef needs?

Ford will sacrifice himself, literally putting both his heart and his life on the line, to protect his man. But will it all be for nothing when Reef is presented with an offer that's too good to refuse?

***White Noise* is book two in Ann Grech's international hit male/male romance series, Unexpected. It can be read as a standalone, but it's recommended that you read Whiteout first. Book 3 continues Reef and Ford's story through the highs and lows of the pro-snowboarding circuit. You'll fall in love and swoon over these two men who are made for each other.**

I was going to dedicate this story to the first responders who are, I think, the ultimate superheros.
And then Orlando happened...
So now, I'm dedicating it both to my superheros, and victims of the hatred. #loveislove – I just wish everyone got that.
Here's to the hatred becoming white noise.

ACKNOWLEDGMENTS

I am truly lucky to have an amazing team of people around me who I can call on for support. To my family – you are amazing. June this year and the lead-up to it were the horror months from hell for me, and your reaction was to give me cuddles, make dinner, top up my wine and cookie supply, and make me laugh when I wanted to cry. I love you to the moon and back— the line out of Toy Story is so much better, but you know, copyright and all that ;-).

My friends who have helped out making Reef and Ford's second instalment a reality – thank you. Kariss Stone, Sassie Lewis, Susan Child, Willsin Rowe and Maci Dillon, I couldn't have done it without all of you. I'm privileged to work with such a wonderful bunch of people who I can also call my friends.

When I wrote Whiteout, I had no idea that I would receive such an amazing response. The MM romance community— the bloggers, readers and fans (especially Robyn Corcoran)

—your support and selfless help in pimping, promoting and reviewing was more than I could ever have dreamed of. I hope I've done Reef and Ford justice in White Noise and you continue your love affair with my boys.

Ann xx

CHAPTER ONE

———————

THE TWENTY-ODD HOURS of being stuck in cattle class sucked. Sitting next to a dude who hadn't showered in a month and stunk to high-heaven was Hell. The putrid body odor, mixed with the sweet body spray the man was using to mask it was making Ford Wallace nauseous. Next time he made the trip from Queenstown to Calgary, he was paying for the damn upgrade. Surely this shit didn't happen in first class? And if it did, well then, he'd be sitting in a recliner with free booze rather than crammed in between two other people on the long-assed flight.

At least he was flying halfway across the world for the best of reasons. That had him smiling in spite of his pity-party for one. Who would have thought that Ford, of all people, would have fallen for Reef Reid? And damn, he was lusting on his man hard. He hadn't had a serious relationship in his life, yet Ford wanted nothing less with Reef. He'd dived in headfirst and couldn't be happier. The best part was he knew Reef felt the same way. His man was in pre-season training, on his way to winning the world championship. Ford knew he could do it and he was damn excited to be Reef's best cheerleader. The last three weeks apart had been fuckin' awful but the flight from hell was coming to an end, the distance between Ford and his man was shrinking. *Finally.* Excitement welled inside Ford; Skype was awesome, but nothing could beat being close enough to touch. Ford closed his eyes, thinking back to the night before he'd boarded the plane.

"One more day, hon." Reef's eyes closed, his words mumbled as he cuddled into the pillow. Ford wanted to be that pillow. Whenever they were together, Reef didn't even use one; instead, he always rested his head on Ford's chest. The chemistry between them was hot, but those moments of tenderness left Ford in no-doubt of their deeper connection.

"Yeah, sweet. One more day. Can't wait to see you, Reef."

"Neither can I. Just wanna kiss you again."

"Is that all you want to do? I want to lie you down, strip you naked and taste every inch of you."

"Mmm," Reef moaned, shifting on the bed. His shaft visibly thick for the third time that night. The man was insatiable — a feeling Ford knew all too well — which was exactly the way Ford wanted him.

"But you need to sleep, Reef."

His man pulled the laptop closer and closed his eyes again. "Stay on with me for a little longer?"

"Yeah, sweet. As long as you want me to." Ford couldn't see much more than his face, but that was fine. He'd called Reef at five in the evening — nine PM Reef's time — and they'd talked for hours. It was two AM in Calgary when Reef finally fell asleep.

"I miss you," Ford whispered, not wanting to wake his man. He kissed his fingertips and ran them over the screen. It wasn't just the sex between them — although that was hot — it was the entire package.

Reef was everything he didn't know he wanted, and now couldn't live without. Ford had stayed like that, watching him sleep for over an hour. He'd fallen hard. There was no doubt in his mind anymore. He was in love with Reef.

The announcement coming over the P.A. system pulled Ford from his daydream. "Ladies and gentlemen, we have now commenced our final descent into Calgary International Airport. The Captain has turned on the fasten seatbelt sign, so please return to your seats and fasten your seatbelts immediately. Your tray tables must be returned to the upright position, your armrests lowered, and blinds raised in preparation for our arrival. Local time is five-fifteen AM, and the expected top temperature is thirty-five degrees with a three inch snow-fall predicted this afternoon."

"Thank fuck for small mercies," Ford muttered under his breath, grateful the flight was coming to an end. If nothing more, he couldn't wait to stretch his legs. His ass had gone numb long ago and the laps up and down the aisle had done nothing to relieve the cramps in his legs, back, and shoulders. Flying sucked, but it was a necessary evil in his life. Living between two continents meant he had at least two long-haul flights each year. Now that he'd be following Reef around for part of his competition season, Ford would be doing even more. And strangely enough, he was looking forward to it. Any chance to see his man, support him and cheer him on was pretty damn good with Ford.

AS FORD PUSHED through the doors into the arrivals lounge, he scanned the room for Reef. He spotted him leaning against a column, one foot up against the wall, his hands in his pockets. Reef's gaze locked with his and it took every ounce of strength he had to stop himself from sprinting across the room and tackling him. Ford's wide grin was matched by Reef's shy smile as he pushed off and stepped toward him. They met halfway, but Reef's gait wasn't that easy relaxed stance Ford loved so much. Yeah, he loved everything about this man but it was obvious something was off, especially when Reef made no move to get in his personal space. Something he normally didn't hesitate to do.

"Hi," Reef murmured, smiling again. "You made it."

"Yeah, finally." Ford nodded, running his fingers through the knots in his plane-mussed hair.

When Reef awkwardly shoved his hands in his pockets, Ford's confusion bloomed. *What's going on?* Was exhaustion making him read more into Reef's body language? His smile and the warmth in his gaze told Ford he was happy to see him, but the toeing of his boot against the linoleum floor and hunched shoulders screamed awkward. Were they back to hiding?

Ford got it, he really did. He'd had to work through his own shit the morning after their first night together. He'd been in his kitchen questioning whether he even wanted to go down the path of being with Reef — the first and only man he'd ever been attracted to. Their chemistry wasn't the problem; he wanted Reef with a need like he'd never experienced. It had lit a spark in Ford which crackled then exploded into a wildfire that couldn't be doused. It was the hurdles bisexual men had to deal with every day – not to mention the way he'd seen himself up to that point – which had made him second guess everything. Ford found himself having to decide whether to give Reef up. But there was no way he could do it, no way he could walk away from the man who'd instantly caught his attention and held it. Ford was inexplicably drawn to him. When he'd come to his senses and was just about to rejoin Reef in bed, Trent had crashed through the door. His homophobic workmate had then witnessed Reef walking half-asleep and buck-assed naked to the bathroom. Everything had turned into a crap-shoot; Ford's careless words hurt Reef and Reef did the one thing Ford couldn't bring himself to do — he walked away. Ford wasn't sure if he'd ever see him again. Knowing it was his fault; his stupid comment that had caused Reef's misunderstanding had almost destroyed Ford. The fact that he couldn't fix it while they weren't talking was like a direct hit to his heart. Sadness, frustration, anger, and finally determination to get his man back had Ford pushing aside anything that could get between them; prioritizing Reef so he understood he was anything but 'nothing' in Ford's mind.

Standing in a crowded airport not having seen each other for weeks, especially after their intimate late night conversations, this no-touching thing Reef had going on was bullshit. He wanted a hug from his man, no he needed one. Ford straightened his spine, forcing a confidence he didn't really have in the moment. It was time to prioritize *them* again. There was no fucking way Ford had travelled across the world to be with Reef if they were going to hide. Slumping down again, Ford let out a frustrated breath. He had no control over Reef's decision; if he wanted to keep their relationship quiet, it was up to him. Ford's only options were to out them — which he'd never do to Reef — or walk away. And that was the last thing he was going to do.

In that moment, Ford finally understood the self-doubt he'd forced on Reef with his attempt to defend their relationship to Trent. The shoe was on the other foot, so to speak, and didn't that just suck. Like the bitch insecurity is, it ripped through Ford, stripping him of all the confidence he'd had in their relationship. Was it his fault? Had it finally dawned on Reef that Ford wasn't good enough for him? Had he unknowingly failed Reef like he had his father?

Ford's knees started to buckle, giving out under the weight of his insecurity. Reaching out for Reef, he did the only thing he could — he pulled him into a hug, desperately needing the warmth of Reef's lean body against him. Ford wanted to bury his face in the crook of Reef's neck inhaling his sent and never letting go. He bit down on his tongue to stop himself from begging Reef to thread his fingers into the curls at the base of his neck. It was Reef's favorite place to hold onto him and in the couple of months they'd shared in New Zealand, Ford had come to crave that touch. Reef went in for the stiff, awkward manly back slap before pulling away. Ford's heart shattered; *he* was *Reef's* dirty little secret. *Or is it even worse than that? Are we over? Fuck.*

Schooling his features to protect what was left of the gaping hole in his chest, Ford pulled away and stepped back. "So, where are you parked?" he asked, his voice devoid of emotion.

"Ford—" Reef pleaded. Worry colored his features, his brow creased and voice laced with desperation.

"Don't. Just don't," Ford snapped.

He turned and Reef reached out grasping his forearm. The touch sent a zing through him that only served to piss him off even more. It was either that or let the broken, jagged pieces of his heart gut him from the inside. Fighting back the hurt he clenched his jaw shut, and shook his head slightly.

"Let me explain."

"Explain what?" Ford spat back, stepping into Reef's personal space and glared at him. "That I've just sat on a cramped fucking plane for twenty hours to come and be with you so you could pretend we don't even fucking know each other? Or what about the fact that I left everything to be with you? And now..." he trailed off, running out of steam as he was faced with the possibility of voicing his fears.

"Keep your voice down," Reef hissed. "There's a fucking reason why I'm acting like a dick. Let me explain in private."

"Fine." Ford motioned for Reef to lead the way. *It'd better be a bloody good excuse.*

Reef led them quickly through the terminal, veering around the one woman who'd caught his attention and not in a good way. Dressed in a neat pantsuit and winter boots, her heavy coat was dropped haphazardly at her feet. It wasn't until they were walking past her that he saw the camera she was discreetly holding, the shutter on the SLR closing rapidly as she snapped shot after shot. What the hell? Why were they being photographed? Ford glared at her not appreciating the intrusion into his private moment with Reef but she was unfazed, looking at him curiously, almost like she was analyzing him.

Pushing through the double door entrance to the parking lot, the blast of cold air hit Ford like walking into a wall of ice, chilling him to the bone. It was a stark contrast to the heated environment of the plane and airport. Reef placed a hand on the small of his back and guided Ford through the trucks and SUVs, stopping at a dark red Tahoe. Quick as a flash, Reef pushed him against the back door of the truck and caged Ford in. "Fuck, I've missed you," he murmured before crashing his mouth against Ford's. Reef's soft lips, hard body, the rasp of his stubble and familiar taste had Ford melting into his touch within a millisecond. *No. Hell no, this isn't happening.*

Pushing hard against Reef's chest he tore his mouth away, instantly missing the heat surrounding him. He had to force himself not to reach out again.

"Stop, Reef."

Reef didn't hesitate, blurting out the words in a rush, "There was a reporter in the terminal. She was there to see Caden Lambert arrive but when she saw me, she followed."

"Caden Lambert, the world champ?"

"Snowboarding royalty? Yes," Reef said sarcastically rolling his eyes at the same time. "We train at the same resort. I offered to pick him up but when I found out he was arriving the same day as you, I told him I couldn't get him. Anyway, he's normally already here but he was delayed this year; his mom had breast cancer. They had the funeral last week."

"Okay, that's... well it sucks, but Reef I don't know if I can do this, us, in secret. I get it if you don't want to be seen with me..." Ford hesitated, not wanting to reveal his biggest fear but knowing he had to man up and say it. "I don't know if I can handle it if you don't think I'm good enough."

"Ford, hon, don't let anyone tell you that." Reef cupped his face with cool hands sliding one to the back of his neck and fisting his hair. A full body shudder ripped through Ford. Need fired within him. He pulled Reef closer, yearning for the contact with him.

"I'd never hide you, Ford. I'd never try to hurt you like that. And I'd never think for a second that you aren't good enough for me. Hell, I wonder what you see in me most days but you make me believe I'm enough for you. I'm sorry if I haven't told you as often as I should how amazing you are." The sincerity in Reef's eyes stole Ford's breath. Pressed close together, Reef's strong hands kept Ford from looking away and his gaze never wavered, never broke from Ford's.

Ford slipped his hands under Reef's heavy coat needing to touch his skin, to reassure himself of what he saw in front of him. The smooth, warm muscles of Reef's obliques against Ford's fingers was like coming home; a balm to his emotional turmoil. His man here in front of him loved him in his own way. Without a doubt he knew Reef meant every word he'd just said. "You don't need to apologize." Ford smiled quickly before breaching the gap between them and pressing a kiss to Reef's lips. The kiss, merely a meeting of their lips, was warm, comforting, familiar.

Pulling back after a long moment, Reef licked his lips. "I do if that's what you're thinking. Talk to me. Why are you worried?"

"I... I don't know. Uncertainty, I guess." He shrugged and looked away, hating his weakness.

"Oh, hon," Reef murmured, kissing his throat and fingering the curls at the base of Ford's neck. He nuzzled into the touch, desperately seeking the affection Reef was lavishing on him. "I'm sorry I made you feel like that. I'm crazy about you. You mean the world to me." Cupping his face in both hands again, he added, "Never be uncertain of us."

Reef brushed his lips whisper-soft against Ford's, the touch sending spindles of warmth through his chest like fingers gently cradling his heart. Resting his forehead against Reef's, he whispered, "Why hide then?"

"She was the one who posted pics of Addilyn cheating on me all over the news. She hounded me until my sponsors threatened to get a restraining order against her. Then she spread all those rumors just to make life hell. I didn't want her to hurt you like that. As desperate as I am to kiss you, doing it in public when she was holding a camera would have given her the next cover story. I'm not hiding you, Ford but I won't come out to her."

"I'm sorry," Ford breathed against Reef's cheek. "I'm tired and had a shitty flight. I jumped to conclusions."

Reef didn't answer. Instead, he hugged him close and pressed their lips together. Ford moaned quietly and wrapped his arms tight around his man, deepening the kiss. Their tongues met, lips melded and Reef growled, tightening his grip on Ford's hair as he thrust his tongue deep into Ford's mouth. The pinch of the strands being pulled had Ford's cock painfully hard, pressing against the button fly of his jeans. His hips instinctively ground against Reef's, seeking the pressure and friction he so desperately needed to get off.

Tearing his mouth away, Ford gasped for breath as Reef licked a path along his cheek, Reef's stubble rasping against his own, and down his throat, biting hard on the tendon. Ford shuddered and moaned, his cock pulsing with need. Reef's grip on his hair had Ford arching into his touch, thrusting against long fingers exploring the bulge tenting his jeans. Lightning sparks lit up behind his closed eyelids, his whole body stiffening as Reef yanked open the buttons and plunged a hand into his boxer shorts. Ford couldn't help the moan which escaped his lips at the skin on skin contact. Closing his fist tightly around Ford's shaft, Reef pumped quickly, dragging his foreskin up and over his corona before stretching it down. Shudders wracked his body as hard and fast strokes took Ford to the edge far too quickly. "Oh goddamn, Reef," he gasped as he squeezed his grip on the down stroke.

"Have to taste you," Reef murmured as he thrust his tongue into Ford's ear before getting' frisky with his lobe. The mere possibility of having Reef's perfect lips wrapped around his cock had him choking out a cry. He instantly missed the heat of Reef's hard body as the other man fell to his knees and wrapped that talented mouth around the crown of his cock. He sucked hard as his tongue did the same frisky move with Ford's slit. Pre-cum leaked from his shaft as his balls drew up tight with the magic of Reef's touch. He handled his body like a master musician plays a finely tuned instrument, each note a crescendo, only to up the ante with every touch which followed. Ford watched as Reef nibbled his foreskin, taking it between his lips and tugging before licking around his head and delving deep. Ford's shaft tapped the back of his throat. Long rhythmic pulls combined with Reef rolling his balls in his palm had Ford sucking in breaths through clenched teeth as he tried to hold back the orgasm careening toward him. Spearing his fingers through Reef's dirty blond spikes, he let his head *thunk* back against the window of the Tahoe. Ford's hips danced in time to the bobbing of Reef's talented mouth. Before he was ready to give up the cavern of Reef's hot wet mouth, Ford's orgasm crashed through him. Each pump of semen deep into Reef's throat sent shockwaves through his body.

REEF LET Ford's sated cock slip from his mouth as he stood and wrapped his arms around him again, holding him close. Three little words were on the tip of Reef's tongue, but how tacky was that? Telling Ford he loved him while the other man was floating on a post-orgasmic haze was not what Reef wanted to do. But Reef couldn't deny that having this man in his arms again brought those words to the fore. Every time they'd spoken on Skype or texted — since he'd left New Zealand — Reef wanted to tell him. Well, that wasn't quite right either. The words had almost tumbled from Reef's mouth when Ford told him about finishing his season at The Remarkables early and joining him for his pre-season training at Fernie, a few hours outside of Calgary.

They'd sat on the banks of Lake Wakatipu in Queenstown, Reef straddling Ford after partying it up at a club where Ford had introduced him as his boyfriend. As they sat together, Ford broke the news that he was joining Reef in Canada. That was the first time he'd wanted to say it. Sure, he known earlier, but he hadn't been brave enough to say the words until that moment by the water.

And now his grand plan of greeting Ford at the gate as he stepped off the plane with a hot-as-fuck-kiss had been shot to hell. Fucking Cordelia Simons. That damn reporter had nearly screwed his life for the second time. Reef had already known Addilyn, his ex, cheated on him. She confessed when she'd called to break things off. But two days later, seeing pictures appear on the cover of every gossip rag showing her at her finest — kissing her lovers goodbye, barely dressed in anything more than a sheet and one or two images of her in the act — was even worse than hearing about it. How the reporter had managed to get over the twelve-foot fence, past the alarmed security cameras and into Addilyn's compound, while dodging her two vicious-as-shit German Shepherds, still surprised him. The photos of Addilyn bent like a pretzel while the photographer she was fucking at the time pumped into her could only have been taken from inside the yard. The thicket of trees surrounding the whole house hid the estate from all the neighbors and even a telescopic lens couldn't reach through the dense forest.

Of course the story started out showing Reef as the victim and Addilyn as the cheating ho she is, but it quickly changed when Reef wouldn't comment to the reporter. Addilyn, desperately trying to claw her way out of the hole she'd dug for herself did interview after interview on how horrible and neglectful a person he was. It was Cordelia Simons' spin on Addilyn's interviews which had Reef looking like the bad guy; accusing him of having pushed her into not one, but into three other men's arms because of a complete lack of affection that bordered on abusive.

Seeing that damn reporter had ruined his plans. All Reef had wanted to do was wrap his arms around his lover and kiss him stupid, giving him the greeting they both needed. But that would have given her the next chapter in the juicy saga she'd created from his life. There was no way he was going to let Ford be on the receiving end of the shit storm he'd been through with Addilyn.

With the taste of Ford's essence on his tongue, Reef leaned closer to his man and kissed his throat, holding his head in place to give him access to nibble on the tendon running down the column of his neck. He'd missed his smell, his touch, the tenderness Ford loved on him with even if he was fucking him into the mattress. He'd missed the warmth of his body lying next to him and their happy times. They were always grinning like fools and laughing at each other's smitten expressions. There was no doubt in Reef's mind that Ford was in as deep as him.

"You've made my day a whole lot better, sweet cheeks," Ford murmured. "And not just for the bloody fantastic blowjob." Reef's chest swelled with pride and not because of the blowjob comment. He loved being the one who made Ford smile especially after he'd had a long, shitty flight.

"And it's gonna get even better. I'll get us to the town-house and you can eat and have a sleep while I meet with my trainer and get a few runs in. I wanna try landing a new trick I've been working on."

CHAPTER TWO

REEF'S MUSCLE memory kicked in as he launched himself from the thirty-foot high precipice. It was a good thing too; the memory which hit him dissipated his focus in an instant.

"Aww, that's so cute." A woman spoke from behind Reef.

Ford stuck his head out from around Reef's body and laughed. "Can you get a shot of us?"

"Sure." Whoever it was said, laughing again. "Ready when you are."

"Pash me, sweet cheeks," Ford whispered, moving close to where he hung upside-down on the set of monkey bar. He'd been doing inverted sit ups attempting to work off the tub of ice cream they'd chowed down for breakfast. Laughing, Reef puckered up.

"Not like that. Kiss me properly, sweet." Ford's voice dropped an octave and using his fingers to cup the back of Reef's neck, he slanted his mouth and joined their lips. Reaching around Reef mimicked the action, speared his fingers through Ford's hair and holding him in place. Lips pressing softly together at first, Reef opened at Ford's tenta-

tive lick. Knowing someone was watching and taking photos had Reef laughing self-consciously as he tried, unsuccessfully, to will the beginnings of his boner from their audience. Running his hand down the length of Ford's chest and abs, he steadied his shaking hands. His man's kiss was electric; pure passion unleashed even when it was chaste. Ford's moan as he deepened the kiss had Reef chasing his tongue as it thrust in and out of Reef's mouth. Hints of minty toothpaste remained, mixing together with a whole lot of Ford. Reef was addicted. Hooked. Ford was like his favorite drug of choice. And he was ravenous for a fix.

"OOMPH," Reef grunted as he underbalanced, landing on his ass then star fishing onto his back and sliding out of control down the steep slope.

He'd landed heavily, coming out of the spin he'd added to the fourth backflip he'd just completed. He got mad air, but his head wasn't in the game. *Head, back, arms, legs. All okay.* Shaking out of the less than stellar landing and unstrapping his helmet, Reef took a deep breath. Damn it, he'd nailed the jump; the parabola of the arc was perfect. The landing angle was in that sweet spot; he should have skied down the slope to cheers of his trainer, instead of...

"Reef, get your head back in the game. Where the fuck is your concentration?" Mason, his trainer shouted as he tossed his helmet aside. Mace was the former European champion. He'd been retired from competition for a few years now, training Reef and Snowbird, another teenage prodigy who'd already won the under sixteen North American championship. He didn't stand for slip-ups like that.

"Sorry, dude. I zoned out," Reef mumbled as his trainer stomped over to where he was lying flat out on the snow.

"You're gonna break something a few weeks out from the start of the season, man, and that'll be the end of it. You might as well kiss the championship goodbye now. What's got you so distracted?"

"Head rush had me thinking of something. Sorry, stupid mental slip."

"Who is she?" Mace asked flopping down next to him.

"Huh?" Reef, was momentarily confused by the *she* part of the question.

"Don't play dumb, Reef. I know that just-laid look. I saw it on you whenever you hooked-up with *the cheating bitch*. Who. Is. She?"

"My lips are sealed. You'll find out soon enough, but not yet."

Mace shook his head. "Reef, I need you to have a good think about this. You're recently single. You've just had some time off, and if you knuckle down and train like a motherfucker, this could be a world championship season. How badly do you want this piece of ass? Is she worth a world championship?"

Sitting up, Reef narrowed his eyes at his trainer, his words coming out a lot harsher than expected. "Dude, don't lecture me. I'm not an idiot. I know the stakes. I get that I need to concentrate and I fucked up, but don't tell me who I can be with and can't. Got it?"

Mason lifted his hands in a gesture of surrender. "Just puttin' it out there."

Reef popped up from the snow-covered ground; standing with his fists clenched, he ground out, "Don't, okay. I've got this."

"Make sure you do. We have to share the bowl — and the pipe — with Lambert now he's here. Don't fuck around." Mason slowly stood, taking his time brushing the snow off his heavy ski pants. Reef didn't bother, the flakes stuck to his clothes would fall off as he moved. Taking a deep breath, he tried to gain control over the sudden burst of anger which had flared within him. It was the pristine white slope dotted with thick strands of trees heavily laden with snow that calmed him. This was his home, his sanctuary. There was no way he'd let Mace rattle his zen in the one spot where Reef was more connected to the universe than any other — his sacred place.

When he was ready to speak again, he muttered, "Dude, I said I was sorry. I'm going for another run. Make sure you're recording so we can pull it apart."

"When am I not recording?"

REEF BOARDED over to the chairlift so he could get a ride up the slope and ski across to the bowl he was training in. The best part about being based at Fernie was that even during peak season the slopes were quiet. Now, before the start of the official season when there was only a handful of people training at the resort, Reef almost had the run of the mountain. The only disadvantage of the place was that he hated training with the six-time world champion, Caden Lambert, around. Caden freaking Lambert was Reef's Achilles heel. The dude loved to gloat and it always put Reef off his game and his game wasn't going to be real hot if his latest slip up was anything to go by.

He unclipped his boot from its binding and let the chairlift collect him. Leaning back, Reef tipped his face up toward the sky studying the weather. Clouds had gathered over the mountain, the wind picking up as a storm system moved in. It'd be snowing for the next few days; now was his last chance to get in a bit more training time. Visibility was turning to shit, so he needed to hurry up or he wouldn't be able to record his passes. The chill had started to set in too but Reef's lips tipped up. He loved the bite of cold weather.

Reef's cell chimed in his jacket pocket. Reaching in, he fished it out, his smile instantly spreading over his face as he read the message from Momma Bear.

Can you still make supper tomorrow night? I'm cooking your favorite.

He typed out a quick response:

Yup, but will there be enough for four? I have someone I want you to meet.

He switched off his cell. He was gonna kick ass on this jump.

STANDING at the top of the run, Reef psyched himself up clearing his mind of all distractions. Eyes closed, he tilted his head to the sky and took a deep breath letting it out slowly as he'd been taught to do in yoga classes. Adjusting his goggles, he focused on the slope, mentally calculating the speed and trajectory needed to achieve a high enough arc. If he got it right, he'd have enough time in the air to execute the four backflips and final rotation before landing a few hundred feet further down on the slope. It was a big jump, a brave one to attempt and he was so close to mastering it.

"You've got this, Reef. You can do this," he encouraged himself. One final glance down double-checking his bindings were secure he pushed off, knees bent, arms down by his sides as he leaned forward to pick up speed. The machine ploughed ramp— cut into the slope a third of the way down the mountain— flew toward him as his almost frictionless board floated over the powdered snow. Quick as a flash, Reef's mind calculated his trajectory. He could do this. This was *his* year.

Launching off the precipice, the rush of adrenaline hit him. Grabbing onto the board, arching backward Reef kicked his legs over his head. One flip. Two. Three flips. The white of the slope and the gray sky rushed past him faster than he'd ever experienced. On the fourth backflip, he changed the angle of his grip and pulled out only to rotate sideward. He'd done it. He'd pulled off the jump. Elation filled him and a wide grin spread across his face. *Fuck yeah!*

Straightening, Reef braced for the landing: knees bent, arms out wide, curled at his elbows. He touched down, momentum propelling him down the mountain. Fighting against gravity — which was trying to pull him onto his ass — Reef shifted his weight forward. Directing his board left then right in wide arcs across the bowl, he slowed down spraying the powdery snow into his trainer's face as he pulled up in front of him.

Reef barely had his neck-warmer pulled down and his mouth uncovered before Mace launched himself at him, jumping on top of Reef and landing them both on their asses all the while shouting joyfully. "You nailed it, buddy! Well done, man, I'm proud of you."

"You got it?" Reef pointed to the cell still in Mason's hand as they laughed and high-fived one another.

"Yeah, dude. Fuckin' perfect jump. You were movin' so fast. The flips were awesome, worthy of Olympic gold. And that landing? Damn perfection, I tell ya. Couldn't find a fault with it. You pull that jump out when you need big numbers, and your season will kick ass. You'll win the whole fuckin' championship. Lambert won't stand a chance."

"Right on."

"Go home and get laid, my man. Whatever you're doing with that girl, keep doing it. I'll see you tomorrow for a yoga session, yeah? Then Saturday back on the snow once this weather's moved through."

"Sounds like a plan. You comin'?" Reef motioned to the building at the base of the ski field.

"Yeah, let's go."

———

REEF STRIPPED out of his jacket as soon as the front door to the townhouse closed behind him. Warmth surrounded him, the fire burned brightly in the main room that served as a combined living and dining off a galley kitchen. The aroma of the casserole bubbling on the cooker had Reef's stomach rumbling. He stripped out of his wet boots and ski gear, taking off everything except his thermal pants and long-sleeved tee. Leaving it all in a pile on the floor in the entry room as he moved, he scanned around looking for Ford. Spotting him standing at the stovetop stirring the thick meaty stew had those warm fuzzies — the ones he'd experienced ever since meeting Ford — fluttering around in his chest. Coming home to him made Reef smile. *This* is what made him happy. Not the accolades of his job, not the sponsorship money, not the travel or even the chance to ski the world's best mountains. Those things were hella fun but having Ford gave him something deeper, something far more meaningful than any of that.

"Hey, you," Reef murmured against Ford's throat as he wrapped his arms around his waist, nibbling the soft skin behind his ear.

"Mmm," Ford hummed reaching behind them and

running his fingers through Reef's hair. Reef ran his hands down to Ford's hips grasping them tightly as he ground his thickening cock into Ford's ass.

"Whatcha doin'?"

"I was cooking. Now I'm thinkin' about the tub. Lying with you like that first time," Ford gasped, dropping his head back against Reef's shoulder as he licked the pulse point on Ford's throat.

"Tell me more." Reef thrust again, teasing the man before him through the thin layers of his thermals and Ford's sweat pants.

"Naked together, after you'd carried me for hours. So brave, saving me. Wanted to kiss you, lick you." Reef closed his eyes and remembered back to the cabin where they'd been trapped for three nights while the blizzard raged outside. When the storm cleared, they'd trekked for hours on their way to the pickup point. Reef shuddered at the memory of Ford losing his footing and being swept up by the avalanche that roared through, decimating the slope they stood on. Panic swamped Reef as a cold dread sat heavy in his gut while he performed mouth-to-mouth, desperately trying to revive Ford after digging him from the snow. The memory of finding Ford's unconscious and injured body still haunted him.

Reef's muscles ached, lightheadedness setting in from the strain. His steps faltering, he was exhausted, struggling to stand with Ford's weight on his shoulders. But he wasn't going to fail Ford. So close. They were so close. He needed to get Ford to safety, needed to care for him.

Wandering away from the filling tub, Reef looked down at his sleeping partner. He was okay. Running his thumb over Ford's cheek, he resisted the urge to kiss him. Barely. Every time Reef closed his eyes, he relived Ford getting torn away from him and fear overcame him. What if he'd lost him? No, he couldn't think like that. Ford was here. He was safe. It was just a matter of time until Mountain Rescue came to get them. Reef had activated the GPS on Ford's watch twenty minutes ago. Now they just had to wait.

Reef pulled away needing to check the tub before he broke down and cried like a baby. Taking a deep breath he tried to center himself, doing the same thing he did before he attempted every competition run. The water was nearly high enough that Ford could sink down into the water and ease the bruises covering his body.

"Couldn't keep my mouth off you," Ford continued, his growled words pulling Reef out of the haunting memory.

"Wanted you so bad too." Reef closed his eyes again, trailing his lips up Ford's throat to his jaw turning his face to capture his mouth. Slipping his hand under Ford's shirt, he tweaked his man's nipple as he punched his hips forward.

Ford pushed his ass back and Reef ground against him ripping a moan from each of them. "Wanted your mouth on mine," Ford gasped. Reef obliged, kissing him slowly, their tongues stroking, lips melding together. Wrapped around Ford and kissing his man, Reef was complete.

"Was desperate for you to do this," Ford whispered between heated kisses.

"Want you," Reef moaned, punching his hips forward again.

"Yes," Ford hissed. Reef pulled the drawstring on Ford's sweats before pushing them down over his hips.

Ding Dong the witch is dead. The wicked witch is dead sounded from the cell phone sitting on the countertop in front of them.

"Fuck," Ford moaned. "Not now, Mother." He pressed

wildly at the screen to silence it before pushing it carelessly away from him.

"Okay?"

"Uh-huh, don't stop." Reef grasped Ford's hips in response and pulled him back against his pulsing shaft.

———

DING DONG the witch is dead. The wicked witch is dead.

"Fuck me," Ford groaned again, slamming his fist against the overhead cupboards. "She doesn't quit."

"Get it, hon; we've got all night. S'okay," Reef replied kissing his shoulder and stepping away to get a bottle of water from the refrigerator.

"Urgh," he grunted. Picking up the cell, Ford swiped his finger reluctantly across the screen before answering, "Hello, Mother." He couldn't hide the disdain from his voice.

"Hello, Stratford. Why didn't you answer my earlier call?"

"I was busy, Mother, I apologize. Did you manage to get tickets?" Ford reached out and took Reef's hand in his, drawing him into an embrace.

"We did, however, I still don't understand why you wanted us to travel all the way to Canada so urgently." Ford rolled his eyes, causing Reef to grin.

"I told you, Mother. There's someone I want you to meet. We're together in Fernie." Ford paused and smiled up at Reef, squeezing his hand before leaning into his chest. "I don't know when we'll be together again. We're both travelling a bit over the next few months."

"Alright, if she's special to you then your father and I

can fly out. I'm happy that you finally seem to be settling down. I just hope you've done your research."

Lifting his head off Reef's shoulder his brows furrowed, he asked, "Research? What are you talking about?" Without realizing it, Ford began pacing the small kitchen.

"What sort of family is she from? Is she suitable as a wife?"

"Mother, I... God, I'm not even going to justify that question with an answer." Ford's reply was indignant. Angrily he added, "Text me the details of when you get in and I'll collect you from Calgary. We're a three or four hour drive away."

"That's not necessary. We'll have a driver collect us and take us to the chalet. We have a lovely home close to yours."

"Fine. I need to go. I'll see you when you get here." Saying goodbye to his mother, Ford hung up and scrubbed his hands across his face. "Un-fucking-believable. Is she suitable?" he muttered under his breath.

Ford didn't see Reef but he could hear the shower running. *Fucking mother.* The woman drove him insane. And she was cock-blocking him from across the other side of the world. *Not fucking happy.*

CHAPTER THREE

Steam floated out of the open bathroom door, as Ford stepped in the doorway listening to Reef hum. He'd recognize that sound anywhere — Reef was content, happy. And so was Ford. He watched the soapy water cascade down his lover's body. Arms resting against the tiled walls, Reef held his head low and Ford admired the view. His muscled back, tight ass and lean legs tempted Ford to strip and join him. It wasn't exactly a hardship to do that either. Ford tugged off his black Henley and stepped toward the shower just as Reef dropped his hand and shut off the faucet shaking his hair out. Ordinarily he'd be disappointed but Ford just wanted to be close to him, to touch him and rediscover every inch of this man's body.

He picked up the fluffy white towel from the nearby hook and held it out ready to wrap around Reef. "Come on out here, sweet cheeks. Let me look after you."

"Mmm, you spoil me," he murmured as he stepped into Ford's embrace, Reef's back to his front. Reef tilted his head back, resting it in the crook of Ford's neck, the wet strands of his blond hair tickling Ford's bare shoulder. Breathing deep, he inhaled the fresh clean scent of Reef's shampoo: the outdoors and that essence which was uniquely Reef. Together it was Ford's favorite smell.

"No more than you deserve." Ford ran the towel down Reef's shoulders and arms. Rubbing his back, Ford dropped a kiss on the pale skin as he moved around to Reef's front. He gently dried Reef's hair, massaging his scalp through the material. Tugging it off, he moved the towel over Reef's chest. This was what he needed; to be caring for his man. A warm glow blazed through his chest, right over his heart.

As he swiped the towel gently over Reef's skin, Ford followed his path with kisses, reacquainting himself with every muscle and plane of Reef's body. Dropping to his knees, Ford dried Reef's legs and feet, before kissing each of his muscled thighs, the soft hairs tickling his lips. He struggled to resist the temptation to bury his face into Reef's groin and run his mouth over every inch of him. Instead he stood and with Reef's hand in his, guided them toward the bed.

Reef nuzzled into him as Ford wrapped his arms around his man, drawing Reef into his embrace. They laid like that, Reef's head on his chest, their legs wound around each other as Ford breathed in the smell of comfort and home. God he was so happy it was sickening.

"Wanna tell me why your mother's ringtone is from the *Wizard of Oz?*" Reef asked quietly.

"Cause she's pretty much the Wicked Witch?"

"You're gonna tell your parents about us?" Reef asked dropping a kiss on his pec as he tickled Ford's oblique with barely-there touches of his fingertips.

"Yeah. I asked her to book some flights over. She and Father are arriving week after next."

"Cool." Reef's tone spoke volumes and contrary to what he said, he wasn't cool about it.

"Is it?"

Reef propped himself up on his elbows and looked down at him, breaking their head to toe connection. "You don't have to tell them, Ford."

"I want to. But is it cool with you? You sound nervous."

Reef looked at him through wide, surprised eyes. "Are you serious? Of course I'm freaking out about it." He held out his fist, counting on his fingers as he spoke. "I'm meeting one of the most highly respected surgeons in London, he's ridiculously smart and has such high expectations for you. Even if I managed to somehow satisfy every other one of their demands in a partner for you, I'd fail the most important one; I'm a man for fuck sake. That isn't gonna make 'em happy, Ford. Yeah, I'm nervous."

Ford pulled Reef back onto his chest, holding him around his waist. Reef held onto him like a lifeline, those strong hands gripping him desperately. Ford covered one of Reef's hands with his own and said, "I don't give a flying fuck what they say, what they think, what they want. I want *you*. Not the anorexic society wife they would choose if they had the chance. You. Smart, strong, sexy, fuckin' talented, manly *you*. This is just a part of us growing together, sweet, not the defining moment for us."

"What if it is? I asked Momma Bear to set another place for dinner on Saturday. Now I'm nervous about that too, about what they might say. I love this, what we have," Reef paused and motioned between them, "But what if it's not enough?"

His arms wrapped tight around his man, Ford begged Reef to understand how cherished he was. Ford wouldn't give him up without a fight and he wasn't a quitter. "It'll only fail if we let it, Reef. And I'm not prepared for that to happen. I told you that we're permanent, that I'll always hold your spot and I meant it. Will you hold mine?"

This time there was no hesitation in Reef's response, no underlying uncertainty. He meant what he said. "Yeah. Yeah, I will."

"Mmm," Ford hummed, rolling them over so he was lying on top of Reef. Joining their mouths together, Ford stroked Reef's tongue with his own, their lips melding as Reef wrapped his legs around Ford's waist. Kissing him slowly, Ford ran his hands over Reef's toned muscles as the other man tangled his fingers into Ford's hair. He was in heaven, couldn't get enough of their connection, the closeness.

"Let me love on you, Reef."

"God yes."

———

THE TIMER in the kitchen roused them, naked and satiated lying in each other's arms. "Ignore it, hon," Reef mumbled, burrowing deeper against him.

"Can't, sweet. Supper's ready."

"But I don't wanna get up," Reef whined playfully, hugging him tighter.

Rolling over so Reef was lying on his back, Ford hovered above him and murmured between kisses, "Stay here, I'll dish some up and bring it in."

"Let's eat by the fire instead. I'll grab the comforter."

"Sounds good." Ford kissed Reef again before stepping off the bed and slipping his sweatpants back on. As he was leaving the room, Ford tossed over his shoulder, "Oh, and don't bother putting any clothes on."

"Ay ay." Reef laughed, saluting him.

Ford sauntered down the corridor, an extra spring in his step. It wasn't just the orgasm — although two in one day was pretty awesome — it was Reef. Having him close, being with him, loving him. Yeah definitely loving him. He had no idea how it was possible in a matter of a few short months or why it'd happened with a man, but it was real. He'd never even had a hint of interest in another but whatever the reasons were, they didn't matter. He was with Reef for the next six weeks and he was gonna make use of it. After that, he'd fly to Italy for the season there and Reef would begin his attempt at the world championship title flying all over the world. They'd be separated for most of the northern winter which sucked but they could make it work. They *would* make it work.

"You excited about starting work, Ford?" Reef asked from the other side of the counter, wrapped in the comforter he'd pulled from the bed while Ford ladled the thick stew into bowls for them.

"Grab the bread?" Ford nodded to the fresh loaf sitting on the counter. Reef picked it up, following him to the thick rug in front of the fireplace.

"Yeah, I've got induction for the next day or two and after that I'll be on the slopes. Can't wait to get up there. They looked so good from here. I love ski-in, ski-out fields."

Reef spread out the comforter on the floor and sat down. True to Ford's instructions, he was buck-naked. Ford tossed him the throw blanket off the sofa before sitting down next to him and taking a spoonful of the tomato and red wine casserole.

"It's heaven up there and there's hardly anyone around. I was the only one on the bowl today."

"No kidding?" Ford replied with his mouth full.

After Reef had shown a little more restraint and swallowed his food, he answered Ford. "Yeah, it rocked. Will you be okay to start tomorrow? Jet lag would kill me trying to do that."

"I'm okay. I might be feeling like shit after I sleep for a few hours but at least I'll have an easy couple of days coming up. Most of it'll be watching safety videos and checkin' out the maps of the slope." Ford shrugged. There was nothing he could do about the jet lag. He'd jumped at the chance to work at the same resort Reef was training at. When the resort director told him his start date, he hadn't argued even though he knew he'd be dead on his feet for a few days. As far as Ford was concerned, it was the opportunity of a lifetime.

"How was training?"

"Nailed it." Reef grinned, his face lighting up.

"What? The jump you've been practicing?" Ford couldn't hide his enthusiasm. Reef had been working on that jump for weeks trying to perfect it and had a few heavy landings in the process. To hear he'd nailed it? Ford was thrilled.

"Yep, triple backflip and a spin on the fourth. Landed it perfectly," he beamed proudly.

"No shit." Ford smiled back at him, practically bouncing in his seat with excitement. "God, I'm fuckin' stoked for you. That's amazing. Hey, did you record it?"

"Yeah, hang on." Reef placed the bowl on the floor in front of him and hopped up, loping over to the counter with a hell of a swagger to collect his cell. Returning to their cozy spot on the rug before the roaring fire he handed the phone to Ford. "Take a look. I've got more footage on my *GoPro* too."

Ford hit play and watched Reef hurtle down the mountain toward a jump set up about a third of the way along the slope. The moment of launch had Ford drawing a breath of anticipation. Three backflips and a perfectly executed spin before Reef straightened and flawlessly landed. It was beautiful, awe inspiring even.

Ford's mind was blown. He'd never seen anything that daring before. Looking up at Reef wide-eyed, he stuttered, "Wo..." He couldn't even get the word out.

Reef grinned and launched himself at Ford. He barely had time to put down the bowl he was holding in his other hand as he collapsed backward under Reef's weight. Still looking up, he grasped Reef's waist as his man leaned down and planted a hard, quick kiss on his lips. "Thank you, that reaction means everything."

"Reef," Ford moaned before connecting their lips together again, gently this time. "So proud of you, sweet cheeks."

"I nearly busted myself up landing the second to last jump. Started thinking about the day at the park when that lady took our pic. Got distracted and I didn't land it. Slid half way down the slope on my ass."

"You're not allowed to do that. I need you in one piece. This body," Ford ran his hands from Reef's shoulders down his legs as far as he could reach, "is too damn sexy to get all busted and bruised."

"I promise, I'll concentrate from now on. Having you in my bed without me being there was a bit of a distraction." Reef brought his thumb and forefinger together, leaving only a sliver of a gap and repeated, "Just a little."

———

THE ONLY GOOD thing about Ford being stuck inside

during his first two days at his new job was that outside it was bone-chillingly cold and being on the slope would have sucked donkey dick. A weather front moved in the night he and Reef slept in front of the fire and had stuck for two days. So induction was painful but at least when he'd gone into the windowless room, it was miserable outside. Reading over safety manuals and pouring over maps of the ski field while sitting in a warm meeting room was bearable. But the videos were just torture.

"Oh fuck me," he moaned, scrubbing a hand over his face. "If I see one more of these movies telling me how to resuscitate someone when I'm already a fuckin' paramedic, I'm gonna lose my shit."

A laugh sounded from the doorway and Ford nearly fell out of his chair in fright. "I'm surprised you lasted this long, Ford."

"Cathy, hi." Ford stood and held out his hand to shake the managing director of the resort. "Shit, sorry I don't mean to complain, I'm incredibly grateful for the job. I really appreciate you letting me come on board. I'm just not used to being stuck inside for so long."

"If I realized they had you in here watching this stuff, I would have come down sooner. Turn it off, you don't need to watch any more. You're more qualified than the person giving the presentation."

"Thank God." Ford turned off the TV and tossed the remote to the side. "So—"

Cathy pointed to the map still spread over the table. Circling her fingers over one of the remoter parts of the resort she showed Ford where the blue line of an intermediate run intersected with the advanced black diamond course. She explained, "Even though this section is well-signed, we find a lot of moderate skiers accidentally end up on this run." Moving her fingers along the mountain, she tapped the part of the bowl showing an almost vertical elevation. "This is a drop off which most people are scared shitless of when they first see it. I need you to do a few hours up here." She once again pointed to the intersecting point of the paths, before continuing, "Just to make sure no one ends up in the wrong spot. Like I said, it's well signed so I don't expect that you'll need to do very much but we like to have someone up there anyway. With all the powder on the slope it's a lot busier today than it's been this week, so gear up."

"The weather's cleared?"

"Oh yeah, wait 'til you get out there. You'll love it, eh." Ford broke out into a wide smile. *This is what I'm talkin' about.*

SITTING on the chairlift was strange. It'd been a long time since he'd worked at a ski resort in a position other than mountain rescue. He normally had the benefit of a snowmobile, and his ever-present medical pack. Instead, he had a bunch of spare maps he could hand out to people. The career diversion would piss off his father — according to him, if Ford was going to waste his time on a mountain instead of a hospital, he should at least be heading up mountain rescue operations. But Ford was ecstatic, already loving every second of this new job now that he was outside. The cold wind made him heady, the prospect of helping people out when they were having fun, rather than injured was a change he was looking forward to. And Cathy's endorsement felt good.

Turning around after hopping off the chairlift to face down the slope, Ford let out a low whistle. The view was stunning. Glittering white slopes fell away before him. There were so few tracks through the powder that they looked almost untouched. Lines of trees intersected the runs, creating wide pristine highways for the skiers to travel along. In the distance, white-capped mountains soared into the big sky, a bright blue after the snow storms had passed. This place was a hidden gem, a diamond in the rough. It was paradise, better than any tropical island could ever hope to be. Cold air fanned across his skin as he dug his poles into the ground and leaned forward, leveraging himself into a glide across the fresh powder. Reef was right, it was heavenly, and being sent to the very same bowl Reef was training on a few days earlier had his excitement ramping up more. Would he be out there practicing again? He was definitely on the snow somewhere but it was a big mountain. The chances of them running into each other were pretty slim. Still, Ford was acting like a teenager, giddy over his first crush.

"HI GUYS, ENJOYING YOURSELVES?" Ford asked the two men who skied up to him.

"Yes," one replied with a heavy German accent. "Which way is the blue slope?"

Ford pointed out the different intermediate runs and warned them of the black diamond run nearby. He offered them a map before waving as they skied off. It had been pretty much like that for the three hours he'd supervised Cedar Bowl — relaxing and fun.

Ford watched the latest group of skiers go past. They'd been up and down a few times already and were obviously familiar with the mountain. The family of three looked to be having a good time. The little girl led the way, followed by her parents who trailed the slope a little more sedately if you could call it that.

The father, an older man that was a little rotund but not obese, waved happily and called out a greeting to Ford in a strong Canadian accent as they neared him. The little girl was much closer and Ford grinned and waved back to them before high-fiving her as she careened down the slope close to him. Looking like a marshmallow, she had the control only a snow baby could have and her form was flawless. Ford kinda envied her skills. Dressed in pink from head to toe, she had to have been put on skis from the moment she could walk. She was adorable. His kid would be exactly like that.

Woah, what the fuck? My kid? But as Ford thought about it for a moment more the idea grew on him, making him smile. *Yeah, my kid.*

As he looked back down the slope a hundred or so yards away, he saw the older man slow down, falling behind the two other members of his group. As he stopped for a breather, he landed heavily in the snow. Ford skied over to check on him. When he arrived by his side, the man was red-faced and was rubbing his jaw like he was in pain.

"How are you feeling, Sir?"

"Something's wrong." He rubbed his shoulder this time as Ford pulled his handheld radio from the pocket of his jacket.

"Base, this is Ford at Cedar Bowl. Come in."

"Reading you, Ford. Proceed."

Ford helped the man out of his skis as he spoke. "Standby for a possible Mountain Rescue call please."

"Standing by, Ford. Over."

"Sir, what's your name?"

"John."

"Hello, John, I'm Ford. I'm a paramedic. May I examine you?" When he nodded, Ford continued, "Are you in any pain?"

"My arm and chin. They're tingling like needles stabbing me."

"Any chest pain?"

"It's hard to breathe. I'm dizzy."

"Okay, let's get you lying down." Ford reached out, grasping the man below his arms and helping him lie down. "Don't worry, I'll look after you. I'm going to check your pulse now, okay." Ford partially unzipped John's jacket as he checked him over. The man was panting, but that wasn't too out of the ordinary for an unfit skier. Especially one who'd come part way down an intermediate slope while trying to keep up with an energetic kid. His lips were pale, almost blue, which combined with the other symptoms concerned Ford. But he was good at hiding that from patients; his poker face was a skill he'd developed as a first responder in London and later the Gold Coast in Australia where he'd worked for a few years. Pressing his fingers to John's throat to check the pulse in his carotid artery, Ford counted out the beats. His heart was a little slow, not racing like you would expect of someone who'd exerted themselves. It was irregular too. *Not good. Shit. Heart attack? Stroke? Another brain condition? God, it could be anything.* Ford ran through treatment options in his mind. Even if he had his pack with him, there was nothing he could give the man without specialist testing. He needed to get the man to a properly equipped emergency department ASAP.

"Base, this is Ford. Mountain Rescue required on Cedar Bowl stat. Code Blue, Code 99. Repeat, Code Blue, Code 99." Taking his finger off the button to the radio, he spoke to the man, "Help is coming. We're going to look after you."

"Ford, this is Base. Acknowledged. Sending Mountain Rescue now. ETA twelve minutes," crackled through the radio.

"My family," John panted, struggling to breathe.

"I saw you with them. I'll alert the guides to meet you at Base."

John nodded as his eyes drifted closed, breathing hard. In a flash, the man clutched his chest and cried out. *Heart attack.*

Ford hadn't removed his fingers from John's throat, still counting out his pulse. His heartbeat had slowed significantly and was more erratic than before. His heart was arresting. *Fuck! Where the fuck is mountain rescue? I need a defibrillator.*

Then it stopped.

His heartbeat gone.

"Fuck," Ford swore, ripping the zip to John's jacket the rest of the way open. Pressing the palm of his intertwined hands to John's chest he began CPR. Chest compressions followed by breaths into his mouth. Ford watched John's chest expand each time he blew a breath in, before quickly changing back to chest compressions. *Where the fuck are they?*

"Come on, buddy, you aren't done yet. Come back to your family. Your little girl needs you," Ford encouraged as he pushed down on the man's chest. Despair shot through Ford before he fought it down and focused, zeroing into a zone of concentration. Every part of his own body was on high alert, his mind cataloguing and interpreting every cue John gave him — the way his breath was forced out of his lungs as Ford compressed his chest, the growing blue in his lips, his slack muscles and limp arms.

"Dude, everything okay here?" a woman on a snowboard asked as she skied up.

Without looking up at her, Ford replied, "What's your name?"

"Kelly."

"Kelly, I need you to take over mouth to mouth for me. Can you do that?"

"I have no idea what I'm doing."

"I'll guide you. Get in position on your knees on the other side of him and I'll talk you through it."

"Um, okay."

Ford swapped to his patient's mouth, breathing for him in two long exhalations. "Get yourself settled. When I get to thirty, you breathe." As she fell to her knees and pulled off her gloves, Ford kept his instructions up while mentally counting out chest compressions. "Tilt his head back, hold his mouth open, then when you're about to exhale, pinch his nose. Breathe when I tell you." Ford continued the compressions, watching Kelly move his head into position. "Don't keep his nose pinched while you wait." Ford kept going. "Twenty-seven, twenty-eight, twenty-nine, thirty, breathe," Ford pressed down again and releasing his compression, he instructed, "Again."

Kelly joined her mouth to John's a second time and breathed out, expanding his chest fully before pulling away and watching as Ford pushed down, manually pumping his heart.

"Well done, Kelly. That was perfect."

The two of them continued, trying to resuscitate their patient. "Come on, John. You need to fight, mate," Ford ordered the man as he checked his pulse again. Nothing. Ford's heart constricted. If he lost this man, his family would lose a father, a husband. Ford needed to step up, to bring him back. It wasn't enough, he wasn't good enough. Ford's father's words echoed in his mind — the criticism when he refused to follow in his footsteps and become a surgeon, then the ridicule as he took his hard earned skills across the world when he'd had enough of his parents' interference. Losing this man would just prove his father right. The old man would love it knowing that Ford had failed in the most spectacular of ways.

The sound of a snowmobile had Ford snapping back from his morose thoughts. "Kelly, stand up and wave them over. Wherever they are, that's Mountain Rescue."

"Hey, hey over here," Ford's helper yelled, waving her arms in the periphery of Ford's vision.

Stopping the snowmobile near to them, the paramedics jumped off and moved toward them. "I need a defib, he's got no pulse. He was in fibrillation but arrested. Suspected cardiac arrest, but symptoms could indicate a possible stroke. No pulse for," pausing, Ford checked his watch before he kept talking, "ten minutes now but I was with him when he went down. I've been performing CPR since." Kelly was already moving back into place.

"You're Ford, right? The new guy?"

Without looking up, Ford answered, "Yes. Twenty-eight, twenty-nine, thirty," he counted out as Kelly joined her mouth to John's again and breathed twice.

"Okay, move back Miss. We'll take over breathing. What's his name?"

"John," Ford replied.

One rescuer checked the patient's pulse and cut open the man's undershirt while the other applied the clear conducting gel to the paddles, rubbing them together to spread the liquid.

"Stand clear," the paramedic with the paddles said as

they each scooted backward, ensuring they weren't touching their patient. The defibrillator charged and shocked the man, his body jolting with the juice being pumped through it. The paramedic checked for a pulse again, adjusted the setting on the machine and applied the paddles once more. "Clear." A shock pulsed from the defibrillator again.

FORD STEPPED BACK as the two paramedics worked furiously on John. They'd obviously heard through the grapevine that he was a paramedic, treating him like a colleague rather than an untrained guide. Being asked to get the snowmobile in place for John's transportation to base and the waiting ambulance was a lifeline for Ford, one he was only too happy to help with. It was a way the paramedics could give him a break from the physically and mentally exhausting resuscitation without pushing him away entirely. Giving him something useful to do helped fill his time while waiting, usually an interminable stretch of uncertainty. Not knowing was awful; knowing you'd failed to save your patient was worse. Keeping busy made the shift pass by faster, not allowing him to dwell too much on whether the person survived or not.

But this time, it wouldn't be as easy to push through. With every passing minute, the hope that John would wake up as the same person he was before — or even wake up at all — dimmed. Ford had the weight of that reality on his shoulders, the knowledge that it was his inability to revive John which would leave this family fatherless and without a husband. Despair swirled around Ford like a winter's fog. Helpless to save John, loss and pain overwhelmed him. Tears streamed down his face and his stomach turned, acid churning like the turmoil in his heart. The certainty that John wouldn't take another breath, wouldn't tell his family he loved them, wouldn't see his little girl grow up wrenched Ford's heart in a vice. Ford fell to his knees and vomited into the pristine snow.

"Daddy? Daddy?" cut through the quiet of the mountain. Unmistakable panic in her voice, the little girl was obviously frantic as she cut across the bowl looking for her father. Ford stood and moved away from the snowmobile, picking up his ski poles before clicking into his skies again. Ford's poker face slid back in place.

"John, where are you?" the young mother called, frustrated.

"Excuse me, love," Ford called out, skiing over to her so that the snowmobile blocked the view of the paramedics working on their patient. "What's your husband wearing?"

The lady described John's outfit to a tee and Ford knew he had to let her know. His heart broke for this woman. What would he do if he lost Reef? He witnessed Reef's reaction to his run-in with the avalanche in New Zealand and that was before they were together, before they'd given themselves to each other, before they'd fallen hard. "What's your name, love?" Ford asked.

"Stella," she replied, still looking around, searching the slopes for her man. More to herself than anything else, she muttered, "Where the hell is he?"

"Stella, my name's Ford. I'm a guide here." He reached out, catching her arm when she didn't look at him. "Why don't we get out of these skis; take a second so you can catch your breath?" Ford used his poles to clip out of his skis, kicking them aside and dropping his poles.

Ford finally had her attention, but her gaze was filled with panic. "What's happened to John? Where is he? What the hell is going on?" The fear in her voice was escalating and Ford knew he was going to be the one giving her the heartbreaking news.

"Stella, he wasn't feeling well. He laid down and has had an attack—"

"No," she sobbed, bringing a hand to her mouth and drawing her little girl in close to her with the other. "Where is he? I need to see him."

"Listen to me, Stella." Ford cupped her arm gently. When she looked up at him through watery eyes, he continued, "He stopped breathing. We've been working on him, but it's not looking good."

"What do you mean he stopped breathing?" she gasped. "Where is he? What are you talking about? Is he going to live?"

"His heart failed. He stopped breathing. I'm sorry." Ford shook his head. It took all his strength not to break down too. Despair surrounded him. One moment in time, a life gone in a flash and others irreparably changed.

And he'd failed to stop it.

Tears streamed down her face as she desperately clutched at her daughter's jacket. "No," she sobbed. "We need to see him. Please."

"Stella, you don't want your daughter to see him like this. Trust me, love."

"You have to save him. We need him."

"I'm so sorry, I don't know if he's going to be okay. I couldn't revive him."

Stella's features turned as hard as stone in an instant. "You? This is your fault? You didn't save him?" she raged, pointing her gloved finger at him while holding her other arm protectively around her daughter. "You're going to live with this. You're gonna to go to sleep every night knowing I don't have a husband anymore. You're gonna wake up knowing his little girl will grow up without a father." Shouting now, she added, "You fucking bastard. Why? Why didn't you save him?" Letting go of her daughter, she pushed Ford aggressively. He stepped back, palms up in surrender as she pushed him again.

Kelly, the woman who'd helped Ford perform CPR, the same one standing to his side and watching the paramedics trying to revive John, turned to them. She was biting down on her knuckles, wiping away the tears that were falling. Seeing these two women — one a stranger crying for a man she didn't know and the other the love of his life — tore a hole in Ford's heart. He'd failed. He was no good, just like his father had said to him many times. He'd failed in the most important thing in his job— saving a life that needed saving.

"Stop," Kelly cried. "Don't hurt him. He tried. We both did. Please, don't blame him. He tried so hard."

"I'll hold you both to this," Stella spat at them, pointing at them in turn.

"Mommy?" The little girl stepped back, looking at her mother with wide eyes. "Mommy? What happened to Daddy?"

"This man," she raged, pointing again at Ford, "this man killed him."

"Daddy, no," the little girl sobbed, crumpling into the ground. Ford lunged for her before Kelly gripped his arm. He couldn't stand seeing her world ripped apart. Down on his knees, his instinct told him to comfort her, to give her a shoulder to cry on.

"No, Ford. You can't."

"Please, look after your daughter, Stella," Ford begged. "Blame me later. Please don't let her hurt alone."

Ford sniffed and took a deep breath trying to center himself like Reef always did. It didn't work; all it did was flood his lungs with perfect mountain air, air that John wouldn't breathe again. Hanging his head down, Ford rose wearily, trudging to the snowmobile. He looked back on the scene before him. On one side of the snowmobile stood Kelly and a few steps away, huddled together and crying were Stella and the little girl. On the other side of him, sheltered by the bulk of the snowmobile was John, lying completely still and the two paramedics hovering over him. They weren't performing CPR anymore. Instead they were checking the time and writing it up. They were calling time of death. This was no longer the rescue of a patient, but the transportation of his body.

Ford promised John that he'd look after him. And he'd failed. A gaping hole ripped into his chest. John had relied on him to save him, to not let him down, to bring him through this. Ford wasn't good enough to save him. Now Stella would be without her husband and the little girl would eventually only have a distant memory of her father.

Ford took another deep breath and swiped away the tears forming in his eyes. He battled down his emotions so he could do his job again. Moving the snowmobile into place, he removed the backboard so they could put John on it and then strap him to the sled.

"Was that the wife?" one of the paramedics asked as he packed their gear up.

"Yeah."

CHAPTER FOUR

Reef had had a mad training session, but the vibe at base killed off his high the moment he'd come off the mountain. It was subdued, like someone had died. Then his trainer opened his mouth and told everyone to perk the hell up. The sheer devastation on their faces didn't bode well for Mace's comment, both of them quickly wishing the ground had opened up and swallowed them whole. What a way to find out a dude *had* died on the slope. Mountain rescue wasn't able to revive him and called time of death on the slope. The ambulance had transported the man's body to the hospital in town and one of the staff members took the wife and kid there too. Reef was hella glad that Ford wasn't one of the mountain rescue team. It'd kill him to lose a patient on his watch.

Reef had no idea what the stress of a job like that would involve but when they'd spoken — while trapped in the ranger's hut during the whiteout — he could see the marks it had left on Ford

"Yeah, London was... hard. It was five years ago; I'll

never forget it. We were called to a triple homicide and suicide. A dude had been drinking. His wife was on the phone with her mother when he got home. He lost it and killed her while her mother was listening. Stabbed her so many times we couldn't count them. Their eldest — a beautiful little girl — heard her mom screaming and ran out. Her father slit her throat where she stood." Ford's voice wobbled and he took a deep breath. "Their little boy was still in a crib and—" he sobbed, no more words coming out.

"Ford, I'm so sorry." Reef wrapped his arm around Ford's shoulder, lending his support. It broke his heart knowing how much Ford hurt all those years on. Ford turned into him and cried, grieving for a family he'd never known but who'd left an imprint on him.

"So much blood," he whispered. Reef held tighter, comforting him in the only way he could. Two strangers led on a path that saw their lives intersect. Reef knew he was where he needed to be right at that moment. Has Ford ever grieved properly for them?

Eventually the sobs gave way to sniffles and shuddering breaths and Ford went limp in his arms. "I couldn't save them. I tried to help the little boy. I tried so hard but I failed him." His tone was defeated, hopeless.

"No, Ford, you didn't. His father did. His father should have been the one to protect him, to love him and instead he was a monster. Don't take his evil on board."

Ford looked at him, brow furrowed, his head tilted like he was thinking about what Reef had just said. "My shrink told me that I was shifting the blame onto myself. I didn't really get it until now."

Reef smiled. All those book smarts and yet Ford still hadn't made the connection. Squeezing his arm around

Ford's shoulders tighter, he murmured against his temple, "You're a good man, Ford. You tried to help. Sometimes that's all you're meant to do. That little boy died knowing kindness, not evil. You gave him the most important gift of all."

"I couldn't go back after that, you know? Not to London. Every time I walked outside I thought about those two kids; knew they'd never grow up, experience the life I was living. Guilt nearly ate me alive. The three of them were innocent, so innocent. I couldn't work for a while. That probably makes me weak but I couldn't keep it together long enough to concentrate. I had to take some leave to get myself functioning again." Ford blurted the words out and Reef could see how heavily they weighed him down. As he spoke it was like a weight was lifting off his shoulders. Ford sat straighter, his deep voice more confident, more relaxed.

"Then Father started pushing me to go back to school and train to be a surgeon." Ford's inflection changed with those few words. Reef could hear the sneer in his voice, as if it was written all over Ford's face but you'd never tell from looking at him; his features were a mask, the perfect poker expression. "I'd heard it so many times; his bullshit speeches and the pressure he put me under. It was awful, I had to get out of there. I got a visa, jumped on a plane and headed straight to Australia. Figured it was about as far away from London as possible. Once I got there, I needed to do something. I was going insane sitting around so I joined the ambulance service as a paramedic. I lasted a year."

"What's the deal with your parents? They seem pretty overbearing on the career thing."

"I told you I come from a line of surgeons. My parents have this ridiculous idea that we're a class above everyone else. Apparently, my duty is to uphold that position and *being a first responder isn't prestigious enough to do that. It's too 'blue-collar'."*

"What? That's fuckin' ridiculous. You save lives, dude. If anything you're better than them. You need a hell of a lot more nous pulling up on the side of the road or wherever to save someone than your old man does in an operating theater."

"God, I wish you could meet my parents. I'd love watching you pull them down a few pegs."

Reef laughed. "It's my specialty. So how'd you end up in Queenstown?"

"Five teenagers went cruising one night and wrapped themselves around a pole. None survived. That was it for me, I was done. My supervisor knew how much I loved skiing and he told me about a job he'd seen advertised for a mountain rescuer. I lasted there for a couple of months until the end of the season and then found a more permanent job in Queenstown. I haven't looked back. And it's even better that Father thinks I'm a bum now."

REEF'S BIRTH parents were flaky at best, neglectful at worst but Ford's parents were a piece of work. They did nothing but cut him down, making him feel worthless even though he was one of the most well respected mountain rescuers in Queenstown. Reef hated them for that, hated them for hurting Ford, for making him believe he was unworthy and Reef hadn't even met them yet. Urgh, he couldn't wait for that meeting. Fun times.

Shuddering at the thought of what would be going through Ford's head if he were the one on the slope, Reef was grateful for the small mercy life had thrown his man.

He'd been through enough already and if the pain the others were so visibly suffering was anything to go by, it wasn't something he wanted Ford to experience again. Reef knew the two rescuers who'd apparently worked on the guy earlier in the day. They were cool, ridiculously nice and damn good at their jobs. He hated the thought that they had to deal with it but if it meant saving Ford from the pain of that loss, Reef would take it.

REEF WAS NERVOUS. Like pacing up and down the hallway biting his fingernails nervous. He hadn't been able to get in contact with Ford all day and now his man was late getting back to their apartment. Was he going to bail on their dinner with Momma Bear and Coach? Reef hoped like hell not but there was no way Reef was backing out now.

The click of the lock sounded and Reef sucked in a breath and mentally coached himself out of the stupid grin he knew he had plastered all over his face.

"Hey," Ford mumbled as he closed the door behind him and kicked off his boots, leaving them where they fell. Reef did a double take. That wasn't like Ford at all. Reef had been in trouble more than once after tossing his boots haphazardly in Ford's laundry room when he'd stayed there.

"Hi, hon. How was your first day?" Reef went over to him and grasped his biceps gently, ready to pull him in for a kiss.

"I..." he started, his head hung low, shoulders slouched. "Okay."

"Did you hear about the skier?" When Ford nodded, Reef continued gently asking, "Hey, are you okay?"

"I'm fine, Reef," he snapped. "Just... I'm fine."

"Okay. Listen, if you're tired you don't have to come tonight. I can head over to Momma Bear and Coach's place by myself."

"No, its fine," he sighed. "Lemmie take a shower and I'll be ready to go."

"Sure." Reef nodded, disappointed at Ford's less than enthusiastic reaction to him. Stepping to the side of the corridor, Reef let him brush against his chest. "Hon," he murmured as Ford walked past him.

"Yeah?" Ford paused, turning to him.

Stepping closer and cupping his cheek, Reef brushed his lips over Ford's. "Cup of tea?"

Ford's eyes fluttered closed and his body relaxed against Reef's as he lightly gripped Reef's hips. Reef pushed his fingers back into Ford's hair tangling in the curls as he hugged him close with his other arm. "Yeah, sweet cheeks. Cup of tea would be lovely."

"Mmm, that accent of yours gets me every time. I missed you today."

"Me too." Ford snuggled down, burying his nose in the crook of Reef's neck. Something was wrong, but Ford didn't give him the chance to question him further. He pulled back, running his nose up Reef's throat as he stepped away. Reef's hands shook. He had a sinking feeling in his gut. It was unreasonable but it was as if Ford was saying goodbye. Reef leaned against the wall resting his foot against the painted surface and closed his eyes, remembering back to the day they did say goodbye, albeit only for a few weeks.

"Last call for Flight NZ620 to Auckland. All remaining passengers for Flight NZ620 to Auckland, please board the airplane from Gate Five, immediately."

"Go, sweet cheeks. You'll miss the flight," Ford

murmured as he held Reef tight to his body, neither of them making any move to let go of the other man. Reef's home was in those strong arms. Leaving Ford's embrace was the hardest thing he'd ever had to do.

"At this point, I'm good with staying here," Reef replied kissing Ford's throat.

"We'll be together in a few weeks. I know it sucks and I'm gonna miss the hell outta you but you've got to do this. You've gotta hit the slopes and practice. I just know you're gonna be next world champion."

"I know I have to go, hon. I just... I don't wanna leave." Reef hugged Ford tighter, pressing another kiss to his throat. Ford did the same thing, running his nose up Reef's throat before pushing him away.

"Go." Ford stepped back one, then two strides. "Go," Ford repeated. Reef nodded and bit back the words that were on the tip of his tongue but weren't ready to be said out loud yet.

"YOU READY?" Ford asked as he passed Reef who was still standing in the corridor in the same place he'd been when Ford had left him to shower.

"Yeah, let's go," Reef responded quietly, nodding his head.

Reef picked up the keys to his rented Tahoe so they could drive the short distance from the mountain village into the main part of town where Momma Bear and Coach were staying for the next few weeks. Ordinarily they'd banter back and forth on the trip or at the very least hold hands in comfortable silence. This time, not so much. It was an awkward, stilted quiet in the truck. Ford clearly had something on his mind and Reef was getting more nervous by the second. How would two of the most important people in Reef's life take the news that he and Ford were together especially if there was a wall between him and his man? Whatever was on Ford's mind was freaking Reef the hell out. Was he having second thoughts?

Pulling in front of the townhouse Momma Bear and Coach were staying in, Reef switched off the ignition and pulled the parking break. In the quiet, he took a second to center himself; eyes closed, deep breath in and out. When he opened them again he looked across at Ford hoping against hope that he'd see reassurance in his gaze. Instead Ford was staring out the window, his chin resting on the heel of his hand. Reef sighed and clicked off his seatbelt.

"You coming?" he asked quietly into the deafening silence.

"Yeah," came the choked response, Ford swiping at his eyes before copying Reef's move and taking off his belt.

"Hey," Reef called out as he interlaced their fingers together. "You can talk to me about it, whatever it is. You know that, right?"

Ford nodded. "I know. We'll talk later."

"Okay. You wanna come inside?"

"I'm not sure about this, Reef." Ford smiled sheepishly.

"I'm a little nervous too. But now or never, huh?"

Ford nodded, unusually subdued. It wasn't like him at all; Reef's stomach pitched knowing something was up but Ford still wasn't talking.

"Let's do this," Ford's strong voice pierced the silence of the truck. Reef looked at him surprised; but it wasn't confidence he saw in Ford's features. It was as if he was psyching himself up, persuading himself that they should go inside.

They stepped out and headed hand in hand to the front door where Reef knocked. Waiting for the door to open was the longest thirty seconds of his life – excluding the minutes he'd frantically searched for Ford under the churned up snow from the avalanche he'd been caught by after their ill-fated heli-skiing trip in Queenstown. It was the beginning of their relationship but it could so easily have ended them before they began. Ford pulled his hand away from Reef's his warm hand gripping the back of Reef's neck instead.

"Sweet cheeks, this is a good idea, yeah?"

"God, I hope so. I don't wanna lose them, but I need to tell them—"

Their conversation stopped short when Coach opened the door and held out his arms. "Reef, son. Good seeing you again. Come in, come in."

"Hi Coach," Reef replied, smiling wide as he stepped into the hug and clapped his pseudo-father on the back before pulling away. He loved this man like his own blood, probably more so. Unlike his own mother and father, Petal and River, who'd win the award for flaky, useless parents of the year, Coach and Momma Bear had been there for Reef through thick and thin. The thought of that changing was terrifying.

"Coach, this is Ford. Ford, Coach."

"Hello, Sir. Pleased to meet you. I've heard a lot about you." Ford extended his hand, shaking Coach's outstretched one. The contrast in their skin tones was pronounced – Ford's pale skin against the deep brown of Coach's African American heritage. That wasn't the only difference Reef noticed either. Coach's skin was wrinkled, the grey hairs starting to outnumber the black. His old man was getting old.

"Is that my boy?" Momma Bear called from the kitchen.

"Yes, Momma Bear. I'm here." Reef grinned. He'd seen her a few days earlier, but these people could always pull him out of any funk.

"Get yourself in here then and out of the cold. I hope you brought the usual with you."

"Yeah, I did." He smiled at Ford who was looking at his empty hands confused as they both toed off their boots and shucked their heavy coats.

Entering the kitchen through the short corridor, he planted a kiss on Momma Bear's cheek, and wrapped the much shorter woman in his arms. He towered over her now, but it hadn't always been like that. The first time he'd met Momma Bear she was the kind, boisterous lady who'd saved his thirteen-year-old ass by organizing a place for him to stay in the ski resort where his first competition was being held. His own mother had forgotten but Momma Bear sorted out everything. Now she was the mom he wished he'd had.

"I missed you, honey. How was practice?"

"Mad. I totally nailed another jump today."

"I'm so proud of you." She smiled, cupping his cheeks in her weathered hands. "And who is this handsome boy?" she asked looking around Reef to his man.

"Momma Bear, this is Ford." Reef couldn't help the warm smile he gave Ford and he wouldn't have stopped it even if he could have.

"Hello, dear. Welcome." Ford reached out his hand to shake hers, much in the same way he'd done with coach but she scoffed at him, pulling him into a hug too. Reef chuckled at Ford's surprised glance at him. Momma Bear had no hesitation in dishing out hugs and by the looks of it, it wasn't something Ford was used to.

"Thank you, Ma'am."

"Such lovely manners but I'm not Ma'am, Ford. Momma Bear is fine."

The table was heaped with comfort food – all of Reef's favorites – chicken fried steak, corn cobs, fresh baked bread and so much more. Momma Bear must have been cooking for hours but that was just her way. When Reef told her she didn't need to make a fuss, her response was always *'When my boy visits, I make a big deal. What kind of momma would do otherwise?'* and Reef loved her for it. Coach fussed with getting them drinks and even Ford was smiling by the time they sat down. Those two never failed to make anyone feel comfortable.

"So," Coach started as they began eating, "How long have you boys known each other? Have you been friends for long?"

Reef swallowed the forkful of mashed potato he'd just shoveled into his mouth before answering. As he savored the taste of the garlic and butter stirred through the smooth potato, he took the moment to think about how to break the news to them. Not that the extra second he took really helped. He'd been pondering how to tell them for the last few days, hell weeks. In the end, he blurted out the basic truth. It wasn't like he'd planned on lying to them anyway but saying it a little more gently might have been better. "A few months now. Ford and I met in Queenstown. We've been together ever since." Ford choked on his food, covering his mouth to stop himself from spitting it out as he glared at Reef. *Oops, a little too blunt.* Reef automatically lifted his hand to Ford's back, rubbing in a circular motion soothing him.

"Wonderful coincidence that you were both training and working in the same place here then," Momma Bear commented. Reef bit back a grin. What a way to pry and

Coach wasn't clueless either. His narrowed eyes told Reef that he knew something more than friendship was between them. Of course, the fact that Reef still had his hands on Ford was a dead giveaway.

"We weren't. Ford got a job over here so he could come and be with me. And once the season starts, I'll be travelling to and from Italy so I can be with him. Is that okay if we work out the itinerary in the next few days, Momma Bear?"

Coach put his cutlery down and wiped his mouth on the napkin he had sitting on his lap before folding it neatly and placing it on the table. Reef knew him well enough to see that Coach had something to say but was holding back. Disappointment painted his features when he looked at Reef. Forcing himself to continue, Reef sucked in a breath. He had to come out and say the words that needed to be spoken; he had to be upfront with them. "I know this isn't what you expected, but Ford and I are dating."

Coach pushed up from his chair and shook his head, then walked away. Reef's stomach dropped and the few forkfuls he'd consumed churned sickeningly in his gut. "Coach, wait. Please," Reef called as he jumped up from his own chair and started to follow the older man. Coach didn't answer as the door to the laundry room closed quietly but Momma Bear did.

"Sit down, Reef. You can't just dump this on us without giving him some time to process it. He wants the best for you, we both do. But is this you? Can you really be happy?"

"Maybe I should go, give you some time." Ford stood. "Thank you for supper, Ma'am. I'm sorry I've upset you both." Turning to Reef he gave him a small smile before stepping away from the chair.

"Ford, no," Reef breathed, hating the wobble in his voice. "Don't go."

"I won't stand between you and your family, Reef. You need them."

"I need you." Reef's eyes were burning, his heart being ripped out of his chest leaving a gaping bloody crater in the cavity. His hands shook as he watched his man shake his head and walk away. Sucking in a deep breath, Reef tried to steady himself, tried to stop the reality that he'd been abandoned once again from surging through him. Resting his elbows on his knees he hung his head low sucking in breath after breath, desperate to stop the tears tracking down his cheeks. Momma Bear stayed silent giving him space to get himself under control again but it was the last thing he wanted. He needed her, needed her comforting embrace. A chocked cry escaped his lips and she was there, her arms around his shoulders rocking him into her ample bosom.

"Oh, honey. I'm sorry, so sorry he hurt you."

"He left, Momma Bear. He knows about my parents and he saw Coach walk out and he just did the same."

"I couldn't do it." Ford murmured from the doorway before coming to kneel before him, his hands gripping Reef's knees. "I couldn't leave you like your parents did. You deserve so much better than that. I'm not good enough for you but hell if I'll walk away from you while you still want me. I'm sorry, Reef."

"I'll leave you two to talk," Momma Bear murmured as she squeezed Reef's shoulder again.

"Thank you," Ford whispered back as his warm hands cupped either side of Reef's face. The smooth pads of his thumbs wiped away Reef's tears as they gazed at each other. Reef leaned into the comforting touch, letting his eyes flutter closed as Ford pulled him closer sealing their mouths together. The kiss wasn't sexual, sensual yes, but not sexual. Comforting, consoling, loving. Reef let his hands wander into Ford's hair as Ford held him tight. Pulling back slightly, Ford kept their foreheads connected.

"I couldn't save him. The skier." Ford blew out a breath and sagged in Reef's arms. "I was with him when he went down." Resting his head against Reef's shoulder his breath caught as he spoke. Mumbling into the soft fabric of Reef's shirt, the heat of Ford's breath against Reef's chest reminded Reef of how very real Ford's anguish was. Reef's heart broke for him. "Everything hit me; all the memories, all the insecurities from my father. Knowing I wasn't good enough to get his heart pumping again, then seeing Coach walk out, seeing you lose him made me want to run so you could keep him." Ford's arms around Reef tightened. "But I couldn't do it." Shaking his head against Reef's chest he continued, "I got up and walked into the other room and left my heart in here with you. Then you got upset and I couldn't abandon you like those bastards did. I'm so sorry."

Reef pulled back and looked at Ford's glistening eyes, the sadness written all over his features. Grabbing his biceps, he shook him. "Don't you ever leave again. You hear me? We're supposed to be in this together but at the first sign of trouble you upped and left." Reef shook his head, clenching his jaw together to stave off his anger. Ford didn't need that being piled on top of him too but Reef was no doormat either.

Looking away, Ford nodded. "I didn't get far."

"Not the point," he mumbled, the wind going out of his sails. They were both hurting and Reef needed his man, needed his comfort. Closing his eyes, Reef drew him close letting the security of Ford's embrace reassure him. Ford calmed him, grounded him in a way he'd never known. Reef brought their lips together again in a soft, slow kiss, cupping his face with his hands. "I'm sorry you lost him, Ford. God I wish you didn't have to hurt anymore. It's not fair." Moving his fingers into Ford's hair, he played with the curls at the nape of his neck as he rested their foreheads together. "It sounds horrible but I was grateful that it was someone else doing the rescue not you." Reef kissed him again, desperate for the small gesture to strip Ford's pain away, to help him heal.

"Even if I had my pack with me, I don't think there was any hope for him." Ford shook his head, tears falling afresh. As Reef pulled back and cupped his face again, wiping the drops away with the pads of his thumbs, he added, "He had a little girl. She was so beautiful."

Reef held him closer and Ford buried his face in the crook of his neck. Shudders wracked his body as he cried into Reef's arms, mourning the loss of the skier. Reef held tight to those curls, rubbing his back with the other hand and kissing Ford wherever he could reach as his man took a few deep breaths and steadied himself.

"You wanna head home?" Reef finally asked, whispering into Ford's ear.

"Didn't want to ruin tonight. I'm sorry it sucked."

"Not your fault, hon."

"You should stay. You need to sort out what's going on with Coach and Momma Bear."

"We're in this together, remember? I'm not leaving you alone. Not tonight."

After a pause Ford added, "Thank you, sweet. I... I need you tonight."

Reef kissed Ford softly once more before pulling back and cupping his face. "Come on, let's go." Ford gave him a small smile and nodded.

———

STANDING HAND IN HAND, Ford looked to the doorway into the kitchen and saw Momma Bear standing there, tears tracking down her own face. "Reef," she sniffed as she reached out to him.

He let go of Reef's hand as his man took her into his arms again. Reef's whispered words against her graying hair were just loud enough that Ford could hear. "I love you, Momma Bear. And Coach. Please don't let this change things between us. Please don't let me lose you."

At that she pulled back and gripped his shirt in both hands. Her words were fierce. "You listen to me, boy. You never have to worry about that. We aren't your blood but we're your family. We will always stand by you." Smoothing out the material, she directed her attention to Ford. She took his face in both her hands. Momma Bear's coloring was similar to Coach's, much darker than his own. "Look after my boy. Love him like he deserves and let him love you. You're a good man, Ford. You're worthy of him."

"How do you know that?" he whispered, uncertainty and confusion swirling around him. It wasn't the thought of loving Reef that scared him. It was disappointing him that was the problem. He'd never been good enough for anyone before, why would it be any different now?

"Because he chose *you* to give his heart to. That makes you worthy." Ford sucked in a shuddering breath again and his eyes filled with tears. "Oh, my boy. Come here." She pulled him close, hugging him in the way only a mother could do. She was right, neither Momma Bear nor Coach were Reef's blood but they were his family. And in that hug, Ford knew Momma Bear was extending that bond to include him.

"You're a special lady, Momma Bear," he sniffed. Ford's

words were softly spoken, just loud enough the three of them could hear. "I can see why Reef loves you so much."

"Don't be a stranger, okay?" she said patting Ford on his cheek.

"Coach might not have the same attitude," Reef interrupted dragging Ford back to reality.

Clipping him across the back of his head gently Momma Bear shook her head. "I'm your Momma, Reef, and I'm telling you both not to be strangers."

Reef's shoulders sagged. Looking at the floor he took a deep breath then spoke the words Ford knew were eviscerating his heart. "I won't come between the two of you. I love you too much to destroy your marriage."

"Silly boy, do you really think you'll lose him over this? You don't know him at all if you think that. He needs time. Give him that. He had a picture in his mind of the lady you'd be bringing home — they're all the same — and as handsome as Ford is he clearly doesn't fit that mold. He had envisaged what your life would be like. You told us so many times how much you wanted a wife and family. Now that's been turned on its head. He needs time."

"I hope you're right. I don't want to lose either of you." Ford couldn't do anything to ease Reef's worry. He wrapped his hand around Reef's arm, lending his support to his man.

"Honey, we'd never ask you to choose. We love *you* too much for that. And once he sees you together he'll know. Now go and spend some quality time together." Then with an entirely straight face she added, "Orgasms help you know. It's a proven fact."

Ford choked and blurted out, "What?" His eyes were bugging out.

"Endorphins, I know." Reef laughed. "You'll get used to her, hon. She has no filter."

"Bloody hell, I can't imagine my mother ever saying that word out loud never mind saying it to me." Ford laughed incredulously. "I'm lovin' what you've got going on, Momma Bear."

Smiling, she herded them toward the door. "Go. Out. Shoo."

Reef unlocked the truck and slid into the driver's side, Ford climbing in the other side. "Sit next to me, hon. Wanna feel you against me." Ford nodded and moved across into the center of the bench seat.

Ford fiddled with the radio controls, turning on one of the local stations as they wound their way through the quiet streets on the road that would lead them back up the mountain and the resort village. Home for now. No, that wasn't true; his home was with Reef. It didn't matter where they were as long as they were together. He'd never experienced the gift of love like Reef's before. His parents' affections were flawed, conditional on Ford meeting their expectations. But Reef's was just there, solid and all-pervading like a sentinel watching over him, grounding Ford and yet lifting him up at the same time. For the first time he was actually beginning to believe he was worthy of that love. Hearing Momma Bear's words, seeing how Reef never let him go when Ford needed him most was like the glue he'd needed to mend the shaken foundations of his love for himself.

Ford instantly recognized the song as 'Taken by the Sea' when it started playing. Darren Hayes was one of his favorite singers. The notes were melancholy and inspirational at the same time but his music always did that for Ford. As Hayes' soulful voice filled the truck's interior, Ford leaned his head against Reef's shoulder, getting as close to him as he could without sitting in his man's lap. Truer words were never spoken — he had hit rock bottom that day and Reef was there to comfort him, to catch him. Reef was his ray of hope, his angel, the light that lifted the darkness around his heavy heart. Reef had started to mend his parents' damage.

"You saved me again tonight, Reef."

CHAPTER FIVE

Reef drew their clasped hands to his mouth and kissed Ford's knuckles. "You know why I'm going so well in training, hon?"

"Because you're practicing?" Ford couldn't help the teasing sarcasm in his voice.

"No, smart ass, it's because of you. You've changed me; I'm a better man with you. This isn't a one-way street, Ford. You give me so much. I'm so grateful for all the things that had to fall into place for us to meet — without even one of them happening I wouldn't have you."

Ford squeezed his hand in reply unable to get any words past the lump in his throat.

When reef pulled into the garage of their townhouse, Ford unclicked his seat belt and made to move out of the truck. Reef's hand on his thigh stilled his movement. "Ford, do you believe me when I tell you how important you are to me?"

Turning to look at him, Ford took Reef's hand in his and

brought it up to his mouth, laying a kiss on Reef's knuckles. "I'm starting to, yeah." Reef's responding smile lit up the car. Ford had fallen hard and fast for that smile. Seeing it again after the lows of the day warmed his heart. Leaning in, he pressed his lips to a still-smiling Reef.

"Come on, let's get inside," Reef murmured, desire flaring in his eyes, darkening the warm brown orbs as he tugged on Ford's hand dragging him out of the Tahoe.

With a hand to the small of Ford's back, Reef guided him through the door first following close behind. Stepping into the dimly lit corridor, they stripped off their heavy coats and scarves as Ford asked, "Do you want a drink, sweet cheeks? I was thinking I might head straight to bed."

"No, no drink." Reef slipped his arms around Ford's waist and Ford relaxed into the strength of that embrace and the love emanating from his man. Even though the words hadn't been spoken, Ford was starting to understand that Reef felt the same way he did. And the squishy sweet feels happening whenever he thought about his man made his cock stand up and celebrate. Ford wasn't even close to complaining; he'd never been attracted to anyone the same way he was to Reef. He'd expected to eventually question his sexuality when he was with Reef but he'd never looked at another man and felt even the remotest pang of longing like he did for Reef. He didn't know what it meant and truthfully, he didn't care what label he attached to himself. Was it only Reef who did it for him? It could be but what difference did it make? Reef made him happy; he found himself smiling for no particular reason other than he was Reef's man. Even his subconscious mind, which would usually be thinking up ways to escape a relationship before it had started, was in sync.

Warm fingers walked their way around his torso and

deft fingers slipped each of the buttons on Ford's black button down free. Using his body Reef steered them toward their bedroom, kissing and nipping the sensitive skin at his throat as they moved. Reef's warm breath on his skin, the touch of his tongue as it darted out to taste, to caress had Ford squirming in his hold, pushing his ass back into the sex-god pressed against him.

Teeth sinking down into his flesh, harder than the other nips had Ford moaning and his cock pulsing against the restrictive denim of his jeans. The need to be closer to Reef was overwhelming.

Reaching around behind him Ford slipped his hand up under Reef's shirt, his breath catching as warm skin connected against his own. Ford lifted his other arm to grasp at the nape of Reef's neck. Holding Reef's head close, Ford angled his own to give his man more room to tease and taunt his sensitive throat.

Their heavy boots thudded down the corridor as they stepped toward the soft glow being cast from the bedside lamp he'd left on. It was intimate in the semi-darkness, just the two of them in a bubble wound around each other. Nothing outside mattered; there was nothing but them. Ford closed his eyes and breathed in Reef's scent: outdoors and man. The now familiar smell had his hardening dick perking up completely. Reef's touch, even through his clothes, lit him up but there was nothing like skin against skin— that was heaven.

Reef chose that moment to skirt his warm palm underneath the cotton shirt Ford was wearing. Pressing his hand to Ford's heart, Reef murmured in a gravelly voice, "Let me love on you, Ford."

"God yes, I need you," he begged as a shudder ripped through his body. He was vibrating, the need to get closer to

Reef, to have nothing between them hummed from his very pores.

When the last button was popped open, Reef dragged the shirt down as far as he could with Ford's hand still clutching Reef's neck, exposing Ford's chest and shoulders to the cool air in the room. He was burning up but his skin pricked with gooseflesh as Reef continued to tease him with delicate swipes of his tongue between sucks and bites on his throat.

Reef's fingers tormented his nipple, plucking at it as his other hand remained pressed firmly against his heart holding him close. There was no doubt in Ford's mind that Reef could feel his thundering heartbeat. But did he know it beat just for him? Three little words begged to be spoken but Ford wasn't ready yet. Not after the shit storm they'd just survived — that he'd just put them through by his failures and insecurities — and not while they were in the middle of sex.

Reef ripped open the button-fly on Ford's jeans, pushing them — together with the black tight boxer shorts he always wore — off his hips. Finally free, his aching cock begged for attention. Lifting his feet Ford tried to kick the pants away but was stopped short when he tangled himself in his boots. Chuckling at his frustration, Reef sunk to his knees pulling Ford's shirt completely off as he went down and tossed it aside.

First one, then the other boot was unlaced and Ford kicked them away as Reef licked along the inside of his thigh, pulling away when he reached his ass. Ford cried out in frustration, craving the touch that would send him out of orbit. His clothes disappeared, everything being thrown in a pile on the floor.

"Reef, I need you," Ford moaned, his voice rough with

desire.

"I know, hon." Reef's mouth connected with his skin again as his palms skirted up Ford's thighs. Panting with need, Ford widened his stance. Reef's touch along the crease where Ford's ass met his thigh had him squirming. Nips along the line of his ass had him moaning and his cock leaking pre-cum, throbbing with want.

The hand pressing at Ford's lower back had him leaning forward. "That's it, hon. Bend right over for me. I'm fuckin' starvin'." As soon as Ford's chest hit the bed, Reef was shouldering his way between his spread legs. When the hand not clutching his thigh wrapped around his cock and pulled it down between his legs, Ford whimpered. He didn't care whether the world outside that room was ending. He craved Reef's mouth on him.

Reef didn't disappoint.

He licked a path along Ford's slit, lapping up the clear liquid dripping from him. The vibrations from Reef's moan shooting straight up his cock had Ford pushing back into his mouth, desperate for more contact. Reef licked the underside of his shaft to his balls and over each one, sucking them gently into his mouth and swirling his tongue around before pushing them out again. Ford clutched the duvet, his hands fisting into the soft material as he buried his face into the covers and moaned loudly.

Reef continued his sublime torture, mouthing his cock and balls until Ford was on the edge. Soft lips, rough stubble heightened every touch. Reef knew him so intimately now, his every move, his every sound that escaped. "Not yet, hon," Reef murmured as he moved to the one place Ford never thought would be remotely sexual but now drove him wild: his taint. With a tongue lashing his hole Ford's vision whited out and need overcame him. "Oh God, Reef, I'm gonna come."

Strong fingers clamped around the base of his cock, halting his orgasm in its tracks. "Hold out for me, Ford," Reef murmured, his deep voice raspy. Spit slicked fingers probed him, opening him and relaxing the tight muscle of his ass. Ford gasped, his back arching as he pushed back against Reef. More, he needed more.

Instinctively, it seemed, Reef knew what he needed, pulling his fingers free before adding more. The burn of the increased stretch made him sigh in ecstasy. Those magic fingers brushed his prostate and Ford's hips bucked forward. Unable to stop himself, he shamelessly rode Reef's fingers while his man suckled every inch of his balls and weeping cock. Ford stiffened again, a full body shudder passing over him as Reef brushed over that bundle of nerves deep inside him once more before pulling free.

"Up on the bed, Ford. On your hands and knees," Reef ordered, his tone rough with desire. There was no arguing with him when he got like this and that suited Ford just fine. He needed something only Reef could give him — he needed to let go completely and fall, to have Reef catch him, to let Reef love on him.

Reef nudged his lubed up and condom-covered cock against Ford's hole. Reef gripped his hip, keeping Ford still and entered him achingly slowly. Popping just past his resistance and holding there, Ford reared back desperate, needy for more. Reef bottomed out in one smooth glide.

There was nothing like it, nothing like the sensation of being filled to bursting and held so lovingly in strong arms. Reef knew every hot button to press on Ford's body, unerringly finding that spot between his shoulders that rocketed him to the edge whenever they made love. This time though, no fingers kneaded his back. Instead those strong arms that Ford loved so much had him wrapped close to Reef's body, pulling him up to sit on Reef's lap.

Ford gasped as Reef sank in deeper and he reached up, gripping the nape of Reef's neck and with his other hand Reef's lower back. Hand on his chin, Reef turned Ford's face to him as he surged in and out, filling Ford and hammering his prostate with every thrust. Ford blinked his eyes open, his gaze locking on Reef's, moaning as Reef circled his hips and pushed even further into his depths.

Reef's index finger ran along his lower lip before plunging in and running down Ford's tongue, Ford sucking on the digit like a desperate man. Reef's hum of pleasure was pure sex, the sound making Ford's balls draw up tighter. He was already skirting the edge when Reef wrapped his hand around Ford's shaft. With one touch he was done for, so overwhelmed by the sensation coursing through his veins that he had no hope of stemming the crashing tide which slammed into him. Like a tsunami, it was unstoppable; a force of nature.

Ford cried out, his orgasm spilling from deep inside, coating his chest with ribbons of warm liquid. He rode wave after wave of ecstasy and floated, secure in Reef's arms as his man found his own release. Shouting out, Reef filled the latex reserve between them; his hips pumped wildly as he bucked into Ford from below. Breathing hard, Ford went boneless, slumping against Reef who was leaning just as hard against his back.

REEF'S ARMS tightened around the man who meant the world to him. He'd left unsaid those three little words niggling inside him, begging to be released. But he hoped his actions showed Ford what a treasured part of Reef's heart he would always hold.

After maneuvering them so Ford was lying down, he made his way on shaky legs to the bathroom. It wasn't the position he'd just made love to Ford in, but the force of the orgasm which had blown through him that left Reef a little off kilter. Tying off the condom and tossing it in the trash, Reef looked at his reflection in the mirror. He had that dreamy, just fucked expression he seemed to wear often these days. Who was he kidding? His sex life with Ford was off the charts hot. Never before had he spent so much time mapping another's body and giving as well as gaining so much pleasure. Ford's scent, the salty tang of the sweat they always worked up on his tongue, the smell of sex in the air — it was hot as hell, but more than that, it was home. It was where Reef wanted to be every night for the rest of his life. This was it for him. Ford was the missing part of his soul, his everything.

The water was finally warm enough to run a washcloth under. Reef wet it and hurried back to their sanctuary, gently swiping the cloth against Ford's chest wiping down the mess they'd made. His napping partner startled before smiling softly and snuggling back into the down pillow, never opening his eyes as Reef tossed the washcloth aside and pulled the warm covers over them.

He tugged Ford back into his embrace once more but Ford rolled over, pressing a leg between his own and wrapping his arm around Reef to hold him close. Heads on the same pillow, foreheads pressed together they breathed each other's air as Reef's eyes fluttered closed. He hummed, pure contentment washing over him. Lacing his fingers into the curls at the nape of Ford's neck, his man sighed and nuzzled their noses together.

"Thank you, Reef. For wanting me," Ford whispered. Reef didn't speak, he couldn't. The only words that would come were the three he was still too scared to say out loud.

After a few minutes of quiet, Ford added, "I'm sorry about Coach. What are we gonna do?"

"I don't know. Give him some space, I suppose."

Ford sighed, nuzzling closer and pulling Reef tighter. "My parents are arriving in a couple of days."

"Oh shit."

"Yeah, I feel exactly the same way."

Reef voiced his greatest fear when it came to Ford. "Hon, what happens if they don't like me?"

Ford pulled back and looked at him. "What, exactly like Coach doesn't like me?"

"No, that wasn't it. It wasn't you. I'm not sure what it was but I don't think it was you," Reef replied believing purely on instinct it wasn't Ford's fault Coach reacted the way he did.

"Does it matter? Even if they don't like you, it makes no difference to me, to us."

"You'll hold my place?"

Ford cupped his cheek and brushed his lips whisper soft against Reef's. "Always." Kissing him again, a firmer press of his lips against Reef's, Ford continued, "Sleep, Reef. You've got training tomorrow."

"Can I train on your slope?" He yawned.

"Anytime." Reef smiled at Ford's reply and kissed him again.

"Night, Ford."

"Night, sweet cheeks."

• • •

REEF AWOKE to the smell of freshly brewed coffee and a blast of cold air as Ford lifted the covers and slid back in. Cold feet pressed on his own had him jumping up and swearing before he burrowed down and gathered Ford close, spooning him to his body. Ford's cold shivers subsided before long but the kisses and nibbles Reef dropped along the nape of Ford's neck and throat had goose pimples being raised on his skin and his man shuddering against Reef's chest. Ford rolled, caging Reef in below him and pressing him into the white sheets of their bed. Reef's legs instinctively fell open, cradling Ford's body against his as he ran his palms up and down Ford's sexy-as-sin lats.

"Morning," Ford murmured against his jaw laying a line of teasing kisses to his throat and back up to his ear lobe, biting it gently. Reef hummed, arching into the touch.

"You made me coffee?"

"Yeah, hon, I did."

"Why naked? It's fucking freezing out."

"Because I knew you'd warm me right back up again." Reef gasped as Ford rolled his hips pressing his growing shaft against Reef's own morning wood.

"Any day of the week. Every day." Reef wound his legs around Ford's trim hips and held on tight as Ford teased and tickled, kissed and licked every inch of Reef he could reach while Reef was wound around him like an octopus. Taking their cocks into his hand Ford fisted them, taking Reef to the edge quicker than he'd care to admit. But Ford could do that — set him off like a Fourth of July fireworks show just by being naked in the same room, no touching required.

"I need you, Ford. I wanna come with you inside me," Reef moaned, barely holding onto his sanity as Ford's now lubed hand worked them over together.

"Fuck yeah," Ford growled, shifting his stance so he could prepare Reef.

"No, just get inside me. I wanna feel you all day."

"I need to glove up, Reef. Lemmie up so I can get a condom."

Reef groaned, frustrated. His skin was on fire, desperation clawed at him. His cock was so hard it was painful.

Primal need overwhelmed him.

As soon as he'd loosened his grip, Ford scooted over and yanked open the nightstand, pulling the drawer all the way out in his haste. The rubbers went flying, the timber drawer dropped to the floor and the lampshade wobbled. "Fuck," Ford growled as he plucked one up and rolled it down his impressive dick. Reef licked his lips at the sight of his man's flushed cockhead, glistening with lube and their shared pre-cum.

"You hungry, Reef?" Ford questioned pumping his fist up and down.

"You have no fucking idea. I wanna suck you off, get you all lubed up."

Giving him that knowing smirk, Ford slowly shook his head as he reached for the lube sitting next to Reef's pillow. The fucker palmed it, drizzling a line along the latex covering his cock as he worked himself over with his other hand. "Oh God, Ford. Jesus fucking Christ I'm gonna come watching you do that." Reef gripped the base of his cock hard, stopping the orgasm ready to crash over him in its tracks.

"Hold your legs up to your chest, Reef. Open yourself up for me." Reef did as instructed, bracing his knees against his chest with each hand and watched, enraptured, as Ford pressed his shaft to Reef's puckered hole. The burn of that initial breach had him sucking in a breath. Ford took it slow, letting him get used to the intrusion until Reef moaned, blissed out. Thrusting in short, sharp jabs, Ford slammed that fuckin' spot within him until he saw stars.

"Oh, fuck. Yes, right there," Reef cried out as his body stiffened. Ford let loose, slamming into him over and over. The only noises penetrating the quiet of the townhouse were their grunts and moans and the slapping of their bodies together. Lightning sparked along Reef's spine as his concentration zeroed in on the desperation for a touch on his cock.

"I'm there, Reef. You with me?" Ford panted as he shifted his weight again, balancing so he could reach for Reef's cock. The touch of Ford's big hand enveloping him undid Reef pushing him over the precipice into the most divine of oblivions. Thick white cum shot from him as his balls tingled and his ass contracted around the hot and heavy cock pumping inside him, a strangled cry ripping from his lips. Ford's shout of completion as he pushed in one last time had Reef emptying the last of his load between them.

Breathing hard, Ford crashed down next to him, trapping Reef's leg under him. A full five minutes had passed before either of them could stop the shaking of their hands long enough to get the rubber off Ford tie it and throw it in the general direction of their attached bathroom.

"I don't think I can move for a week," Reef bemoaned.

"Me neither but I need to go. I'm already pushing it to get to Base on time."

"Sorry, hon, you bring me a coffee and I tempt you into being late." Reef was barely sorry but it was only the second day Ford had been working at Fernie. He didn't imagine his boss would take it too well if he showed up late, especially if he had that just fucked swagger that Ford wore so well.

"Tempt me anytime, sweet cheeks." Ford looked across at him, eyeing him hotly. Reef knew that look. If he let him, they'd be going a second and possibly third round before either one of them stumbled out of bed.

"You need to go to work and I need to watch some film with my trainer so I can get out on your slope today."

"Urgh. You suck."

"And I also swallow. Now get up." Reef tapped him on the ass copping a feel at the same time.

"I'm going, I'm going," Ford grumbled, rolling over and stumbling out of bed. Pointing at Reef, he grinned wickedly. "And I'm getting T-shirts printed that say you suck and swallow. You wait and see."

CHAPTER SIX

"Okay, this bit." Reef's trainer paused the video feed connecting the laptop to the wall-mounted flat screen in the townhouse. Moving close to the TV, he pointed out Reef's posture. "See that? Your knee is bent inwards at an awkward angle. You need to bring your knee out so you don't twist your hips. You'll do some damage if you land like that."

"Yeah, okay. I see it," Reef replied, nodding. He'd felt himself doing it. Now that he could see the mad air he'd gotten and the way he'd landed on their last training session on Mason's video, he knew what he was doing wrong.

"Now look at this one." Mace tabbed through the open video footage on the laptop as he brought up the GoPro recording from Reef's helmet. It was paused at the same point on the same jump that Mace had just played. As he started it, Reef watched how his leg twisted more on the landing and his board slipped wildly nearly making him lose balance. Reef's grunt of pain sounded clearly over the rush of the wind. "Don't let me see you do that shit again or I'm gonna have your girl put you on rations.

You'll be fuckin' horny as well and sore from my foot up your ass."

Reef shifted on the soft sofa, definitely feeling his escapades with Ford that morning. A grin formed on his lips which he had no hope of stopping. "I want you two to meet. Today. We ready to hit the slopes yet?"

"Sure. This was the last of the jumps I wanted to go through anyway." Mason paused, clasping him on the shoulder. "I'm happy for you, Reef. You're happier than you've been in a long-assed time."

"Thanks, man. I *am* happy. It's great, better than I could have imagined."

"So, your girl's a ski bunny, huh? 'Bout time you got one of us."

Reef's chuckle turned into a snort of laughter when he thought about how Ford would react to being called a snow bunny; the man was anything but. He didn't bother answering his trainer. Mason's eye roll was enough to get Reef laughing again.

————

"YEAH, BABY!" Mace shouted as Reef slid to a stop at his feet. "Another rockin' trick and a perfect landing. Reef, you're on fire, my man." High fiving through thick gloves, Reef grinned. Damn he loved his job. Nothing could be better.

"One more run, hey? But this time, you're with me."

"She's waitin' for you is she?"

"Come on." Reef motioned to the T-bar lift at the bottom of the run that would take them toward the larger chairlift that ran back up the slope.

Letting go of the pole, Reef slid away heading down the

intermediate run while he waited for Mason to hop off behind him. A bright blue sky stretched above him, the sun shining caused the snow covered trees and ground to glitter like diamonds. His vision was a weird mix of orange and browns— the lenses of his goggles casting everything with that orange hue. Tugging them up onto his helmet, Reef blinked at the blinding reflection. The beauty of these slopes awed him every time. The trees, weighed down with a heavy covering of snow, piercing the blanket of white was magical especially against the contrasting blue of the sky. Fresh cold air gusted around him, crisp as he breathed it in. Nature surrounded him, the peace and quiet of the ski fields resonating in his soul. The cry of an eagle far above had the memory of pulling Ford out of the avalanche rushing at him. Like a tight fist closing around his heart, the panic of that near loss — one which would have been so incredibly devastating — almost choked the wind out of him. Heart hammering in his chest, he took a deep breath grounding himself in the here and now.

"He's okay. He's alive and yours and in love with you," Reef coached himself. *But is he? He almost walked out. Almost ended them. No, that was to protect me. To give me back Coach. But he hasn't said it.*

Neither had he.

It was time; time for him to tell Ford how he felt. Time for his man to know he was Reef's forever.

His white picket fence.

His happily ever after.

His family.

His love.

Reef grinned. Ford had said he was getting T-shirts printed. Maybe he should get a set too: 'his one' and 'his only' on each shirt. *Corny much? Hell yeah, it's perfect.*

. . .

REEF SAW FORD IMMEDIATELY; even from across the snowy bowl on the mountaintop he stood out. Wearing the traditional black and red that ski instructors around the world seemed to wear, he stood tall waving to a grommet as the kid flew past him. Reef skied toward him knowing Mason would keep up. As they approached, Ford pulled down the neck warmer from around his face and shot Reef a wide smile. Reef's heart skipped a beat and his dick thickened. Smiling back he resisted the urge to... no he didn't. Barreling into Ford he crash tackled him, sending them both sprawling into the snow as he claimed his mouth in a fierce kiss. Skis and snowboards entangled, Mace's shout and the sheer joy of touching his man again had Reef laughing against Ford's mouth. Ford bit down on his bottom lip, sucking on it until Reef's semi was a fully-fledged boner.

"Everything okay, sweet?" Ford asked, concerned.

"Missed you. So fuckin' much."

"So you planned to come and ambush me while I was working?" Ford grinned, the worry lines in his brow disappearing.

"No, I had intended to resist the urge to jump you but then seeing you in that getup and knowing what you're wearing underneath, I couldn't help it."

"Did you hurt yourself? Your trainer's about to kick your—"

"Dude, what the fuck? Are you blind? Are you tryin' to end your season before it begins?"

"Mace, calm down. We've crash tackled each other enough for Ford to be okay with me landing on him."

"Huh?" His trainer looked at them confused, that confusion turning to shock as it dawned on him that Reef had his fingers entangled in Ford's hair and neither was making a move to get up. Their bodies aligned, arms wrapped around each other, faces pressed close. It was a hell of a way to come out.

"This is who has you jumping better than you ever have before?" Mace's grin lit up his face.

"Yeah, man. He is. Ford meet Mason Canning, my trainer. Mace, Ford Wallace my boyfriend."

"Great to meet you, dude." Mason held his hand out to Ford who shook it, still lying down. "I had no idea, Reef. I'm sorry. Shit I've been giving you hell about a new girl and he's clearly not... a snow bunny. Oh, man is that why you were laughing when I said it earlier?"

Reef couldn't help it. He was giddy with the nervous energy that had been released into his system. After Coach's less than enthusiastic reaction to his coming out he'd had no idea how much he needed someone else to be on their side right at that moment. Light from the weight being lifted off his shoulders, Reef laughed then nodded. "Yeah, dude. I was picturing Ford's face if I changed his pet name from honey buns to bunnykins. I kinda like it."

"Don't you dare." Ford was clearly trying to look threatening, but in his position, partly buried in about two feet of snow lying below Reef, he was hardly intimidating. Pressing a kiss to his pursed lips, Reef pushed up onto his knees before rocking back and standing. Stopping his board from sliding down the steep slope, he reached out to help Ford sit up but his man was already on his feet too.

"I might. I might not, bunnykins." Reef smirked at him.

"Smart ass c'mere." Reef leaned toward Ford who gripped his jacket with gloved fingers. Pulling them closer, Ford pressed their mouths together, dipping his tongue inside. He tasted of chocolate — Reef probably did too, the sugar hit gave them the much-needed energy to keep their bodies active. Reef hummed, their tongues tangling as they held onto each other.

"I need to keep an eye out on the slopes but I'm off shift in a half hour. Wanna go for a ski when I finish?"

"I'd love to. I might do a run or two then meet you back here, yeah?"

"Mhmm," Ford murmured, kissing him again before Reef turned and skied down the advanced run Ford had stopped at the intersection of. "You comin', Mace?" Reef yelled behind him as he shot down the steep slope.

As he reached the intersection of the advanced and intermediate slopes he watched as two kids — five or six year olds at most — tried to master the natural jump at one end of the bowl. Mason ignored them but Reef was captivated, instantly picking up what their errors were.

"I'm gonna talk to these kids for a while, Mace. You go on ahead."

"Okay, man. Don't forget you're meeting Ford."

"I won't, buddy. But it's nice of you to say. I'm glad you like him." Reef held up his closed fist so they could bump them together.

"He makes you happy, so what's not to like?" Mace smiled at him but became serious again quickly. "I had no idea that you'd been hiding all this time, Reef. I'm sorry you felt the need to do that. I hope it wasn't anything I did that made you feel you couldn't tell me."

"See that's the thing, I've had a crush on a guy before but not anything I would have wanted to act on. But with Ford, well, I couldn't keep my hands off him. And he's only been with women before me. Never even looked at another man."

"Really?" Mason's eyebrows hiked up, clearly surprised with Reef's admission.

"Seriously. I've never said I'm bi because it wasn't relevant. But now," Reef shrugged, "I can't see myself with anyone else."

Mason tilted his head to the side, considering Reef. "You're in love with him, aren't you?"

Reef gave him a shy smile, embarrassed that he'd been called out. "He should be the first person to hear that, don't you think?"

"Tell him, Reef. Believe me, you don't want to miss the chance."

"Yeah, I'm starting to realize that. When the time is right I will."

"Don't wait too long. Now go and mess around with those kids. I can tell you're itching to get some more air."

"I wanna give them some pointers."

"Yeah? Let's see how well you go doing my job." Mason laughed, crossing his arms over his broad chest.

"At least as good as you, smart ass." Reef grinned at him. He'd missed his trainer and friend during his time in New Zealand. They'd reconnected over drinks the first night Reef had arrived but hadn't had much of a chance to socialize since then. "Hey, when are you free next? We should go out for drinks again."

"Absolutely. Anytime you want. Tonight if you like."

"I'll check with Ford." Reef smiled at the thought of he and Ford hitting the clubs again. They hadn't done that since Queenstown when Ford told Reef he was joining him in Canada. That was a perfect night. Reef would never forget grinding up against Ford to Bruno Mars and then to Charlie Puth's 'One Call Away'. As Ford had pinned him to the bed that night, he'd whispered sweet nothings to him, explaining exactly what the song meant to him.

His fingers were laced with Ford's and Reef was lying trapped beneath him, his arms raised above his head. Ford moved slowly in Reef, their eyes locked, not in a battle of wills but to watch and read each other, to love on each other– Reef loved opening himself to his man. In that moment, Reef had never been more vulnerable letting Ford not only into his body, but into his heart. If he was being truthful, Ford had moved in with earthmoving equipment long before that night and demolished any remaining barriers between them. And Reef had never felt so protected and loved.

"You're my superman, you know that?" The sincerity shining in Ford's eyes stole Reef's breath. Brushing his lips over Reef's ever so gently he murmured, "You saved me. Not only from the avalanche but from myself.

Reef pulled his hands free and cupped Ford's face before kissing him softly. Ford thrust, again, bottoming out and spoke again when their lips were a hair's breadth apart, their foreheads pressed together. "You've given me so much, Reef. You're the only one; the only one who's given it to me."

"Given you what?" Reef asked confused, running his fingers through Ford's curls.

"You." He replied, kissing him gently as he brushed his knuckles over Reef's cheek. "You gave me all of you. Your heart, your body. Everything."

Reef ran his hand down Ford's body, arms and legs winding around Ford in a tight embrace, holding him close. "Kiss me, Ford," he whispered, nuzzling their noses together.

HE LOOKED up to see Mace skiing off down the slope so Reef unclipped one boot out of the binding on his board and pushed his snowboard like he would a scooter over to the boys.

"Hey, guys, nice moves," Reef called out to the kids as he clipped his boot back onto the board.

"I'm Caden Lambert," the shorter one yelled excitedly. *Wonderful, the two people he speaks to on the mountain have to be fans of the world champion.*

"No, I am," the taller boy growled. "I told you."

"Where are your parents, boys?" Reef asked looking around. They were too young to be on the slopes alone. That was something his parents did and he wouldn't stand for others being left to fend for himself like he had.

"Just up the slope. They're coming now. That's them at the top. Our big brother was supposed to stay with us but he saw a girl. He's gone over there with her." The taller boy pointed to the thicket of trees a hundred yards or so away from them.

"Oh, okay. Hey, if you really want to be Caden Lambert you should try this when you hit that lip." Reef demonstrated how to push off the jump from his stationary position near to it.

"Awesome!" the taller boy cried. "My brother's way didn't work."

Reef watched as the two kids ran part of the way up the slopes, lugging snowboards behind them, strapped in and slid down. Their form was spot on, clearly having grown up on a mountain. The shorter boy hit the jump first copying Reef's move exactly, only to get an extra foot of air. Whooping as he landed, he skied over to Reef and high-fived him.

"Go George!" the little boy cried, watching his brother shoot down the slope. Knees bent in just the right way, he hit the jump and Reef yelled his encouragement. The takeoff was perfect but the landing not so much. Stacking it, the taller boy somersaulted a few times before coming to rest splayed out on his back. Reef immediately skied over to him and helped the young boy up, picking up and handing over the beanie which had fallen off his head. Reef couldn't help the wide smile that spread across his face. What a kick.

"Hey, who the fuck are you?" A teenaged boy came sliding up to them, spraying Reef with snow as he stopped his board. "Leave my brothers alone."

"Why so you can leave them alone too? I was making sure they're okay and giving them a tip on how to jump."

"Yeah? What the fuck would you know?"

"You wanna lay off the language? Your brothers are kids."

"You didn't answer the question."

"I don't have to. Don't leave them alone again when your parents trust you to look after them."

"What's going on here?" A man the spitting image of the teenaged boy skied up. Reef looked him up and down. Top of the line everything, all well-worn but in good condition.

"Your son left the kids alone while he went off with a girl. I saw them alone so I came over to make sure they weren't up here by themselves.

"You did what?" the mother asked, horrified. "Anthony, you insisted you were responsible enough. You begged us to leave you alone. I told you not to leave their sides. They're too young to be here by themselves. Anything could have happened."

"I was watching, alright?" he replied mulishly.

"Sir, thank you for stopping to check on them." The father held his hand out to Reef. "I'm James, and this is Cathy, Fernie's resort director."

"Oh, hi. You know Ford," Reef blurted out before he could stop himself. *Oh shit, they probably don't know about us.*

"Yes, we go way back. You know him too?"

"Yeah, we um," Reef hesitated, embarrassed by his slip of the tongue. He wrung his hands together, color staining his cheeks as he laughed at his awkwardness. "We're staying together."

"Really? I thought he was staying with his boy... Wait, you're Reef Reid. You *are* his partner."

"I am."

"It's a pleasure, Reef. You've been training here for years and I don't know how we've never met. If you're not doing anything tonight, you should come to the inn for drinks with us."

"That sounds great, I'll check with Ford. I mentioned to my trainer, Mason, that we should catch up, too."

"I invited Ford this morning. He was going to check with you." Cathy smiled. "Bring Mace too. It'd be great to see him again."

"Alright, that sounds good. Nice to meet you all." Reef waved and skied off toward the chairlift. He was going to be late to meet Ford if he didn't get a move on.

CHAPTER SEVEN

Ford waited for Reef at the top of the run. His shift ended ten minutes ago but it was a good thing Reef was taking a while getting there. He'd had time to look up a T-shirt printer and spoke to them about the designs he wanted. On his he was getting 'You suck.' On Reef's it was 'I also swallow.' They'd never wear them in public but it'd be a hoot having the two shirts. Imagining Reef wearing it, and only it, had his cock perking up and taking note.

"Hey, bunnykins." Reef grinned as he skied up spraying Ford with an arc of snow. Ford scowled, not because of the pricks of cold dotting his skin but at the name. *Could it be any worse?*

"Reef," he sulked pulling off his beanie and rubbing a gloved hand over his head. The cold breeze ruffling his messed up hair as he shoved the beanie in his pocket was refreshing after the warmth of his headgear.

Reef nudged Ford's arm with his own. "Honey buns, remember what you said by the lake that night in Queenstown? You don't choose your pet name, it gets given to you. So don't complain, but I now dub thee bunnykins." Reef spun on the spot still strapped into his snowboard and touched each of Ford's shoulders as if he were knighting him, all the while laughter flashing in his eyes and his lips curled. *Bastard.* Ford remembered. How could he forget? It was one of the best nights of his life. *But bunnykins? Really?*

"Fuck me, you realize how..." Reef's wicked grin and his dimples to die for told Ford everything he needed to know. "Urgh. I'm not gonna win am I?"

"Not a chance." Reef laughed. Ford grunted his distaste and reached up hands above his head to stretch while leaning his shins against the hardened wall of his ski boots. The design of the boots made for a great skiing position, but standing in a crouch all day always gave him stiff knees.

"Here, eat some chocolate," he said to Reef in mock disgust, pulling a couple of Snickers from his pocket.

With a wink and a smile Reef snatched it off him and spoke while unwrapping the bar. "Hey, I ran into the resort director and her family on the slope. That's why I'm late."

"Yeah?" Ford asked, moving closer to Reef and wrapping his arms around his middle, Reef's back to his front. "I told Cathy about you," he murmured as he kissed Reef's exposed throat. "Were the boys with her? I saw them together this morning."

Reef mumbled a, "mhmm," as he swallowed his first bite then continued, "Whole family. Her teenager's a delight."

"Little shit, isn't he? Met him this morning, too." Ford paused, following Reef's gaze as it panned the slope. A wide bowl lay before them falling steeply away. This one was different from the one he was on the day before. The tree line was higher, intersecting the trails in peaks and valleys. Smooth white highways snaked down the slope and in places smaller rocky outcrops formed natural jumps that only the most experienced of skiers could land. At this time of afternoon the fields were emptying, the lifts were gradually closing down and patrons filtering home. It was Ford's favorite time of day. Quiet had descended on the slopes; the departing of the few skiers hollering and whooping their delight left the rustling of the nearby trees, the cry of a lone bird and Reef's steady breaths the only noises to be heard. The snow gods were kind to him gifting him with a job in a place as beautiful as Fernie. Worry slipped away, responsibility evaporated while —with his man— he worshipped at the altar of nature.

"God it's beautiful here," Reef murmured quietly. Turning his head so his ear lay against Ford's jacket Reef nuzzled Ford's throat before reaching up to drop a kiss on his cheek. "Thank you for coming and sharing it with me."

"I don't wanna be anywhere else, sweet." Ford hugged him tighter just as he heard Reef's stomach growl. "Cathy invited us out for drinks tonight. They're going to the inn. It's apparently pretty nice. Wanna go? Maybe we can have supper there, too."

"I'd love to, yeah." Reef nodded. The broad smile he flashed up at Ford was filled with genuine happiness. "Wanna go for a ski first? Somewhere where it's just us?"

Ford smiled, looking out again at the empty slope before them. "Yeah, if we go down this way," Ford motioned. "There are a couple of black runs which are pretty quiet or so I'm told." Reef nodded and extracted himself from his embrace.

They set out down the run together, the rustling of powder under Ford's skies and the rush of wind against his face reinvigorated Ford. Looking across at his man shredding down the mountain, Ford thought of their first time skiing together. It was a hell of a trip— whiteout storm, getting trapped on the mountain for days and then almost getting killed in an avalanche. But it was full of great memories too. They had three uninterrupted days together where he and Reef got to know each other. The attraction between them had sizzled, then Reef had rescued him and it had moved to a whole new level. This was the first time they'd been skiing together since.

"This feels good doesn't it, Ford?" Reef called out to him as the slope leveled out and they neared the end of the run.

"Yeah, sweet, it does. Missed this with you." As Reef slid to a stop, Ford halted close by watching Reef waddle with his feet bound to his board to get closer to him. Ford was riveted, unable to take his eyes off Reef as he reached out and wrapped a gloved hand around the back of his neck pulling him closer. His lips against Ford's were hungry. He opened immediately as Reef licked a line across his lower lip. The man he'd totally fallen for captured Ford's moan. Standing in the powder with the groan of the T-bar lift ferrying people back onto the trails that would lead to Base with his man in his arms, Ford was content, truly happy.

"I—" He'd started to say *I love you* when his cell buzzed in his pocket.

"You'd better get that, Ford. It might be your mom letting you know they're boarding."

Giving Reef a brief kiss he fumbled, pulling his gloves off and unzipping his jacket to pull the buzzing cock-block out of his pocket. *Yep, there goes my libido.*

"Hello Mother," he answered, not letting go of Reef, their bodies still pressed together.

"Hello Stratford," she sighed. "The airline has moved our flight. We will be arriving a little earlier than anticipated. I will send through our updated itinerary. I have already informed the driver, however, I would appreciate you confirming it." She spoke in her clipped tone, the one she used with their staff.

"Sure, Mother. Send it through and I'll call the guy."

"Why do you insist on speaking like a commoner, Stratford? You were educated at the best schools. Please uphold your position, your name. I hope the lady you are introducing us to has a breeding that can appreciate your heritage."

"Goodbye, Mother." Ford pulled his cell away from his ear and hung up before she could continue. He was not encouraging her bullshit. Slipping his cell back into his jacket pocket, he zipped up and reached for his glove as he turned back to Reef. He was pale — as white as a ghost. Ford spoke quietly to him and even he was surprised at how much warmth was in his voice. "Where were we, sweet?"

"There's no hope they'll accept me, is there? I mean seriously, I'm screwed on at least two fronts just from that conversation." Reef threw his hands up, looking away from Ford and trying to waddle backward.

"Reef listen to me," he spoke firmly holding him tight with one arm while he turned Reef's face toward him. "I don't care whether they do or don't."

"But I do, hon," Reef replied sadly. "I can't ask you to give up your family for me. Or your inheritance."

Ford's laugh held no humor. "Even if I wanted their money, I have no doubt that my mother will do her best to spend every penny before it comes to me. I've been nothing but a disappointment to them since day one. Mother and Father are hardly going to hand me the millions of pounds they pretend they have if I'm gonna live like an 'uncultured heathen' as Mother so eloquently describes my choices. I live my own life, Reef. You're in it. Get used to that. They aren't gonna change my mind about wanting you."

"So... we face them together, the same way we did with Coach and Momma Bear?"

"Exactly. But without the part where I freaked out." Seeing Reef trying to suppress his grin Ford knew his attempt at levity had worked. "Did you hear from them today?"

"I messaged Momma Bear. She told me to leave it a few more days before hitting up Coach to 'pull his head outta his ass' as *she* so eloquently described it."

Ford laughed and hauled Reef to him again kissing him with all the love he had for his man. Pulling back, he buried his nose in the crook of Reef's neck. Outdoors and man, Ford's favorite smells, filled his senses. Need ravaged him; Reef naked and writhing below him in blissed out ecstasy was the only thing he wanted — no needed — in that moment.

Reef apparently clued in on the change in him. Moaning he let his head fall back as Ford devoured him, licking and biting the prickly stubble on his throat. "Let's go home. My dick will shrivel up if I take him out in this weather," Reef gasped as Ford bit him.

Grabbing his hand, Ford turned and tugged Reef down the mountain.

———

THE LIVE BAND playing in the inn reverberated onto the street every time the front doors were pushed open with people entering or exiting the bar. Reef had been there before; apparently it was always a good night out. From the way he'd described it, the inn sounded a lot like the sports bar he loved in Queenstown. He wasn't prepared for how much character it had though. Like an old Irish pub back home, it had the exposed timber beams along the walls and roof and the unmistakable smell of hops and Guinness. But it also had a uniquely Canadian feel too — the pool tables and dartboards in the corner, were shadowed by the over-sized maple-leaf flag pinned to the wall. Hanging above the tables was a huge pair of antlers surrounded by smaller ones interspersed with pictures of the colonial settlers and native Indian tribes. Thankfully no heads of dead animals were mounted, but the look and feel of the dark timber and muted lighting gave it a rough and ready feel. Ford loved it instantly.

"Cathy's over there," Ford pointed to a group of small black tables and chairs placed against the stained glass windows near to the bar. "And by the looks of it, Mason's here too."

"Cool," Reef replied, smiling. Waving his hand around the inn he asked, "So what's your first impression?"

"Fuckin' awesome. Love it already. Should we get a drink before we sit down with them?"

"Yeah, let's do that."

They ordered beers and potato skins to start then made their way over to the tables the others were sitting at. Cathy and her husband, Mace, Caden Lambert and his trainer along with a few other people had already arrived. Drinks flowed, the conversation was light — even with Caden's ribbing of Reef's world championship chances — and the food was good. The inn was filled to bursting, music blasting through the speakers. When Ford looked up, a flicker of light caught his attention. The swinging doors to the kitchen closed quickly but Ford's gut told him some-thing was wrong.

"Reef," he grasped his partner's arm and looked over. Reef stopped mid-sentence, mouth open.

"What do you need, hon? What is it?" he asked, instantly understanding there was a problem.

"I don't know, but something's off."

A scream rent the air as a blast of smoke erupted from the kitchen. Feedback screeched through the speakers when the band dropped their instruments after the crowd surged away from the back of the inn.

"Out. All of you, out. Now," Ford shouted, gripping Reef's arm trying to push him toward the door.

"I'm coming with you."

"No, you need to get out, Reef. Please, I need you safe. Take Cathy, get the first aid gear from Base. Get all the people in there. They'll freeze once the sprinklers—" Ford's words were cut short when the sprinklers turned on, drenching everyone in the inn.

"Alright. Let's go everyone. Now." Reef took charge, throwing a table through the nearest stained-glass window and kicking out the shards. People surged at them, and Ford prayed Reef wouldn't get trampled. Smoke was fast filling the inn and the panicked crowd was starting to freak out. Ford jumped up on the nearest table and shouted for people to get down on their knees out of the haze of smoke. The sprinklers were pushing the cloud of hazy air downward, making it harder to breathe, the water rendering his tentative perch on the round tabletop tenuous as hell. The fire alarm screeched, disorienting some of the crowd and making them move in the wrong direction, closer to the flaming kitchen instead of away from it.

"No, this way," Ford shouted over the din, waving them over with one arm as the other covered his mouth trying to filter the thick smoke. It was no use, they couldn't hear him. He jumped down off the table and slipping as he did, pushed against the flow of exiting people to reach the few confused patrons.

Grasping a man's shoulder, he spun him around, pushed him to his knees and shouted, "Crawl that way, follow the others. That's the exit." He did the same with two more people, one of whom was pressed against the door to the kitchen, her eyes wide and makeup streaked in the downpour from the sprinklers.

Soot covered everything, blinding Ford as the water streamed down his face. Scrubbing a hand over it, he pushed back his hair and knelt down, placing his palm on the door to the kitchen. It wasn't hot, but there was heat on the other side of it. No one had come out since the fire started. Was there an escape out the back? He had to make sure there was no one in there who needed help. *Where the fuck are the firefighters?*

Pushing the door open a crack, he peeked through. A fire was curling its way up the wall, the building now alight. How it started didn't matter to Ford, all that did was the building being empty. Crawling through the door, he spied a chef with a fire extinguisher attacking the flames. Ford reached for the fire blanket hanging on the wall and yanked it out of its protective bag. Stepping as close to the cooker as he dared, he threw the blanket at the gas burner.

"Come on, we need to get out," he yelled to the chef. "It's not worth dying for."

The chef tossed the fire extinguisher to the side and stumbled toward Ford. Wrapping an arm around his waist, he propped the lady up as he half dragged, half marched her out of there. After handing her off to the paramedics, Ford turned to head back inside, stopping when a, "Hey, wait," was yelled.

"Is there anyone else in there?" one of the paramedics asked.

"I'm not sure." Ford started coughing, gasping for breath by the end, a sure sign of smoke inhalation. "She was in the kitchen fighting the fire. I don't know if there was anyone else."

The second paramedic took Ford by the elbow, steering him back to the ambulance. "Stay here so the firefighters can secure the area when they arrive. They're less than a minute away. Let me check you out."

"I have to find my boyfriend but I'll come back. I know the drill with smoke inhalation." Ford turned, pulling out of the paramedic's grasp and jogged — as much as he could while hacking up a lung — into Base.

"Reef?" he yelled, slamming through the doors. "Reef? Where are you?"

"Ford? Ford, he's not here." Cathy screeched, wide eyed and panicked. "He wouldn't leave while there were people still coming out of the inn. He was waiting for you. He's still in there. Oh God, get him out, Ford," Cathy begged.

"Oh fuck, no," Ford cried, spinning on his heel and sprinting out of the Base, running across the street back to the inn. Fear, no terror, turned his blood to ice. Nothing in his life compared with the dread coursing through him at the thought of Reef lying injured or trapped in a burning building. He pushed past the firefighters who had just arrived only to connect with a thick arm across his chest.

"Hey, stop. You can't go in there. It's not safe."

"Reef?" he shouted ignoring the man, struggling to break free of his grip. "Reef?"

"Sir, stop," the firefighter commanded.

Ford turned his attention to the man. "Fuck off, I'm going in."

"You. Aren't. Allowed. In." Ford's temper snapped, together with the firefighter's nose as his fist connected with the man's face. Fire radiated up Ford's hand and arm but it was nothing compared to the ache in his heart. He needed Reef to be safe. That was the only thing that even remotely mattered.

Instantly, the man let go of Ford, cradling his nose with both hands. Ford didn't bother to check whether he was okay. The paramedics were already running toward the fire-fighter who was howling in pain and screaming bloody murder at Ford. Instead he ran, hurdling the window Reef had smashed.

"Reef? Reef? Where are you?" he screamed. Panic raised the pitch of his voice as he tipped over tables and chairs looking for his man. Quiet. It was eerily quiet. The fire alarm had been deactivated. The crackles and groans of the building still sounded though, together with the hiss of the water spraying through the sprinklers.

"Ford? Ford, I'm outside. Get back out here," Reef shouted through the shattered window.

"Reef? I'm coming." Ford crouch-ran back out toward the sound of Reef's voice. As he cleared the smoke haze, he saw him. Safe. Waiting for him just outside the window.

Ford stepped over the shattered window, shards of glass underfoot, out to safety. Reef was on him in a millisecond, wrapping him in his arms. The paramedics were by their sides quickly, whisking them toward the ambulances lying a safe distance away and trying to place an oxygen mask over Ford's face.

He batted it away just wanting to feel Reef against him. He held his man tight, burying his face into the crook of Reef's neck. Reef's embrace was just as strong. Ford had never been so relieved. Joy filled his soul, pushing out the dread and terror of moments ago. Having Reef in his arms at that moment surpassed every moment in his history.

Reef's familiar smell was masked by a coating of soot. They were filthy and freezing but Ford was so very grateful they were alive and kicking. "Don't you ever and I mean fucking *ever* do that to me again. You should have left, Reef." Ford growled into his throat, gripping Reef's jacket hard, shaking him in anger and begging him never to give him a scare like that again. Unwilling to let even a sliver of space between them, Ford couldn't see Reef's reaction but he felt him shake his head.

"I did, Ford," Reef said adamantly. "I walked out with the main part of the crowd. I directed them to Base and Cathy took them all there, opening up the doors for them." Reef pulled back, pushing against Ford's shoulders until they were standing face to face. "I got out, but I couldn't leave you in there alone. I had to wait."

Ford shook his head, grasping Reef's lapels. "I came straight out, Reef." Pointing in the direction of Base, he spoke vehemently, "I went across the road looking for you and you weren't there. If the gas supply went up, you could have died, sweet. I can't lose you." The wobble in Ford's voice gave away his panic, the last four words ending on a whisper as Ford crumpled back into Reef's embrace shaking.

"I'm sorry, hon," Reef cooed, running his fingers through Ford's tangled wet hair. "I didn't see you come out. There are people fuckin' everywhere." They stood like that, holding each other tight, reconnecting after avoiding Ford's worst fear. Being tossed around like a ragdoll in a million tons of snow was nothing compared to the terror at the thought of losing Reef.

Taking a deep breath and recollecting himself, Ford channeled his training. "I need to check you out."

"*You* need to be seen to. I've been checked and I'm okay." Ford forced himself to let go and check Reef over himself. He turned Reef's face into the light. His eyes were bloodshot and a slightly swollen. Ford noticed Reef's wince as he looked into the bright spotlight he'd turned his face toward. Reef's voice was a little hoarse too but that could be because they'd been shouting over the din of the music all night. Ford watched closely as Reef breathed; he wasn't struggling. Satisfied, Ford relaxed. Reef was okay. His man was fine.

Ford, on the other hand, was fighting for each lungful of air. Short of breath, he started coughing again. Reef pushed him away, forcing him to sit on the sidewalk. "Hey," he shouted to the paramedic. "He needs help."

The same paramedic who'd tried to help Ford before came over. This time he offered no resistance to the oxygen mask being placed over his face. The paramedic slipped his stethoscope up the back of Ford's shirt and listened to his breathing.

"You're gonna need transport to the hospital, eh. You need a chest x-ray."

"I'm okay."

Reef stood over the top of him. "Ford, you're a paramedic. You know the risks of a self-diagnosis being wrong. You're going to get the damn x-ray."

Packing his stethoscope away, the paramedic kneeled in front of him, shined his pen light in Ford's eyes and doing a visual inspection for injuries. It was a surreal moment of quiet in the chaos around them. Firefighters were tackling the blaze. The smoke pouring from the building had petered off. Clearly their effort to put the fire out was working. People milled around everywhere — some in pajamas and robes — and the noise from the chatter of the crowd almost overwhelmed the generators on the fire engines working to pump water through the fire hoses. The police had arrived moments after the firefighters and in a flash, had cordoned off the area around the emergency vehicles, pushing the press of people back to a safe distance. It was only himself, Reef and the emergency workers who were within that perimeter now.

Dropping his penlight into his bag, Jean the paramedic — according to his nametag — spoke, "Your breathing is already settling down. The x-ray is a precaution but your partner is right. You were one of the last people out of that building. You inhaled the most smoke. You need the x-ray." Reef squeezed his hand and nodded. Ford hadn't realized he'd sat down beside him or interlinked their fingers.

"Fine," Ford sighed. If that's what it took to make Reef happy he'd do it. Didn't mean he wanted to though; he was quickly getting sick of the inside of hospitals.

CHAPTER EIGHT

REEF SAT on the passenger seat of the SUV as Ford turned into the wide driveway of his parents' chalet. The lights hung like lanterns along the cobblestone way lighting their path past the triple garage at one end of the building and onto the brightly lit front of the castle-like house. Ford parked at the foot of the wide staircase leading to the double timber and stained-glass front doors. The two-story stone building was designed in the same style as an old-world French chalet and it screamed money. It was easily three times the size of the townhouse he and Ford were staying in. The sprawling grounds surrounding the charming mansion were so expansive that, even in the center of town, the lights from the neighbors' houses weren't visible. The gardens had an ethereal glow about them from the heavy coating of white lit by the three-quarter moon in the sky. He could imagine what the gardens would look in the summer — manicured to within an inch of their lives, with not a single leaf or blade of grass out of place.

Reef's nerves flared as he double-checked his clothes. *Is this okay? I should have worn a suit.* He looked across at

Ford. They were both casual but Reef still felt under-dressed. It wasn't a feeling he was used to and the nerves sucked. *Urgh.* He touched his hair, making sure none of the errant strands had moved.

"Your hair is fine, Reef. You look fuckin' hot."

He'd spent forever standing in front of the mirror trying to get his usually messy hair to sit with some semblance of order, but no amount of product could tame it. *Is 'hot' what he should look like? Shit. Who knows?* He was blaming Mason for this nervous energy. His trainer had refused to let him do any cardio in the week since the fire even though he hadn't coughed much after that first day. There was no way he was still suffering from the effects of smoke inhala-tion. All sitting around did was serve to turn him into a nervous wreck. Cooped up inside his townhouse, he watched film, did yoga and almost pulled his hair out driving both Mace and Ford insane with his nerves. Nothing worked to calm him down, well except when Ford left him in a sweaty, sated puddle on their bed. But aside from that, his concentration was shot to shit; not even the yoga had helped.

Smoothing down his scarf and wiping his sweaty palms on his jeans, Ford took a hold of his wrist. "Sweet, calm down. It's gonna be okay."

"I can't. I'm freakin' out." Fidgeting, Reef shifted in his seat. Anxiety raced through his system. He'd never once been this tense — not even in a competition — never been so adrift in his life. Heart racing and unable to take anything but short, sharp breaths, Reef's vision started swimming. Ford's finger on his wrist disappeared, replaced with a hand at the nape of his neck, pushing his head down to his knees.

"Long slow breaths, Reef. I've gotcha, you're okay." All Reef's focus zeroed in on the warm palm anchoring him to

Ford. The dizziness cleared as his heart rate and breathing slowed to their normal pace. He mustered every technique yoga had taught him and closed his eyes imagining himself at the top of a peak, the cold wind fanning his face. Thinking about the mountains, the serenity surrounding him when that blanket of white stretched before him, his zen returned and Reef sat up. "You okay?" Ford asked, his hand back on his wrist now monitoring his slowing heartbeat.

"Yeah, think so." Reef looked away, embarrassed.

"Hey, Reef, look at me," Ford implored. Reef took a deep breath and turned in his seat ashamed he couldn't handle the stress. Ford had also unbuckled his belt and was facing him. Taking his face in his palms, Ford pulled him forward so their foreheads pressed together. "Whatever happens in there, we're together. This doesn't change us, it doesn't matter. It's a courtesy to my parents, that's all. I want you; no one else. They may not be happy about us, but it doesn't matter. I don't care about their opinion, I care about you."

Reef held onto Ford's waist like a lifeline. Grounding him, his man smiled and Reef couldn't have turned away even if he'd wanted to. Ford brushed his lips whisper-soft against Reef's and he melted into the touch. "Kinda nerve-racking meeting them, that's all. I don't want to create a bad impression. I want to be good enough for you."

"You are, sweet. No matter what gets said in there, no matter what happens you and I walk out together. We're solid. Yeah?"

"Yeah." Reef nodded, smiling for the first time since they'd left the townhouse.

"Pinkie-swear?" Ford held out his pinkie to Reef, the rest of his hand in a fist, eyebrows raised and a wicked grin curving his lips. Reef snorted out a laugh before curling his own pinkie around Ford's.

"Pinkie-swear it." Turning to look toward the not-so-imposing front door and thinking about the frigid reception he knew he was going to get still made his balls shrivel up. "Let's get this over with."

"That's the spirit. Exactly my thoughts whenever I see the doctor and his wife." Ford leaned in and kissed Reef with a hard press of his lips before pulling away and throwing open the door of the SUV. Reef mirrored his actions and met Ford at the bottom of the stone staircase. With Ford's hand pressed against the small of his back, Reef let him guide them to the door. Before pressing the buzzer, Ford turned to him and smiled, leaning in for a slow kiss.

"HELLO STRATFORD, PLEASE DO COME IN." A lady, who Reef guessed was Ford's mother, motioned for them to enter the chalet. Her perfectly coiffed blonde bob barely moved as she stepped back out of the cold Canadian wind. Dressed in a white calf-length skirt, a pale pink cashmere sweater and white pumps, she radiated old money. She instantly reminded Reef of the Queen of England. Maybe it was just the accent or perhaps it was the way she carried herself. The diamond jewelry she wore — which rivaled the royal crown in cut and clarity — didn't hurt either.

"Mother, how are you?" Ford kissed her on the cheek before stepping over the threshold and unbuttoning his heavy woolen coat and removing his scarf.

When her gaze momentarily flicked to Reef, it was enough for him to see the surprise in her pale blue eyes but it quickly disappeared. Unmoving after Ford greeted her, she held her head high as she spoke, her tone filled with an air of superiority and primness Reef had never experienced before. "Well thank you, Stratford. And you?"

"Stellar." Ford cracked a grin at Reef, warming his heart and easing the tension knotting his muscles.

A little.

Maybe.

Hell, who was he kidding, Reef was a wreck, even more so now he'd seen what Ford's mother looked like. This meeting the parents' thing? Fucking awful.

As they stood in the large foyer taking off the heavy outer layer of clothes, Ford's father entered. There was no mistaking the two were related. If Reef wanted to know what his man would look like in thirty years, all he had to do was check out his father. They had the same bright blue eyes, but where Ford's blues sparked with life and were full of mischievous fun, his father's were cold. Shrewd. Gray hair cropped close to his head and disguising the wave contrasted with Ford's chocolate brown curls, curls Reef could barely get enough of. Ford was sure to develop laugh lines near his eyes and around his groomed stubble. His father's face was unmarked in those spots. Instead, he had a concentration frown currently marring his otherwise smooth face.

"Stratford." Ford's father nodded at Reef's man and shook his hand. What sort of father does that? Seriously, a handshake? They hadn't seen each other for months. Sure, they'd made the trip to Canada at Ford's request, but still. As he observed them, Reef could see evidence of the quirks Ford had mentioned when speaking of his parents. They shook hands like business associates, a healthy distance between them and without any hint of a smile. They presented a united front; Ford's mother stood by her husband's side equally stiff, her hands clasped together in front of her body. While Ford's father ignored Reef entirely, his mother made no effort to hide the disdain in her gaze directed exclusively at Reef. Ford may have a strained relationship with his parents but even Reef expected more happiness in their greeting. What Ford was putting up with was ridiculous. When he'd seen Momma Bear and Coach, he'd been wrapped in hugs all round, his face peppered with kisses from his flamboyant 'adopted' mom. Even his real parents, whom he barely spoke to, showed Reef more affection than Ford's were at that moment.

"Mother, Father, may I present Reef Reid, my boyfriend." *Oh fuck me. Just come right out and say it, Ford. Jesus H Christ.* Reef was sure he wore a look of surprised horror judging by Ford's reaction. The bastard laughed. He actually laughed. Sliding an arm around his shoulders Ford whispered, "Loosen up, sweet cheeks. What are they gonna do? Kick us out? We can go for burgers if they do."

"Pleased to meet you Dr. Wallace, Mrs. Wallace." Reef lifted his hand in a small wave, not brave enough to try and shake Ford's father's hand.

Ford's mother barely hid her sneer as she spat out words which belied her stone cold undertone. "Stratford, why don't you come in and sit down. The chef has supper almost ready. We can have a nice evening together."

"Thank you, Mrs. Wallace. That would be..." Reef fumbled for words. *Fucking horrifying, God-awful? His worst nightmare?* He settled on, "nice."

"Yes, Mother," Ford replied, anger in his voice. "*Reef and I* would love to come in and eat some five star food." Ford's tone, laced with sarcasm, was clearly a warning. It wasn't until Reef replayed her words that he realized she'd only invited Ford in.

"Please, you first Mother, Father. We'll follow you." Ford held Reef back as his parents stepped forward not waiting for Ford to follow. Ford turned his attention to him as he laced their fingers together. He saw straight through the brave façade Reef was trying to maintain. Knowing he'd disappointed Ford's parents without even having had the opportunity to speak to them was even worse than he'd expected. Giving him a sympathetic smile, Ford squeezed his hand. "Reef, it's okay. This is them. They show about as much warmth as a cold fish."

Reef couldn't meet his gaze anymore. Looking down, he shuffled his socked foot. "I'm not welcome here, Ford. Maybe I should go."

"No," Ford's retort was louder than Reef expected. Blowing out a breath, Ford continued, lowering his voice. "We agreed we'd walk out together. I'm not leaving until they understand we're serious. Nothing they say is gonna change my mind about you. Now come on, I'm in the mood for whatever the hell it is the chef has cooked."

"Does your mother cook?"

Ford barked out a laugh. "You're joking right? That's a job for her minions."

"Your parents are really rich, aren't they?"

"Dunno," Ford shrugged. "But they like to project to the world that they are. Don't really care to be honest." Standing in the foyer together, the light of the crystal chandelier cast a warm glow over them. Now that Ford's parents weren't there, the room had taken on a different atmosphere — it was no longer cold, unwelcoming. Drawing strength from Ford's unwavering loyalty to him, Reef smiled and wrapped his arm around Ford's waist, dropping a kiss on his stubbled cheek.

"Yeah, come on. Let's eat. What's the worst that can happen?"

Arm-in-arm, they walked through the grand archway into a reception room where sofas faced a blazing fire. It was ridiculously sumptuous but still had a homely feel. On the other side of the room was another square archway leading through to a dining room set with a starched white table-cloth, white crockery, wine and champagne glasses glittering in the light of the chandelier which hung from the ceiling. Elegant pillar candles on silver candle sticks stood in the middle of the table, strategically placed so the view from the four places set would not be blocked. The deep color of the timber on the chairs was rich, like everything else in the chalet.

Seeing Ford's parents in their element, Reef's nerves flared once more. Holding Ford was never wrong but this time Reef appreciated a little discretion was warranted. He pulled away, putting a respectable distance between them before giving the others an unwanted PDA.

Dr. Wallace was already seated at the head of the table, tasting the white wine a waitress had just poured. Mrs. Wallace was seated quietly to his left but her silence made the tension in the air thick enough to cut with a knife. There weren't many situations where Reef was genuinely uncomfortable but this was one of them. He'd jumped out of planes, skied down slopes so steep they were regarded as unpassable, gotten mad air and landed so many jumps he'd lost count. And yet, the rapid beat of his heart as it smashed against his chest, the lightheadedness, and his sweaty palms told Reef just how nervous he truly was. Normally, he didn't care about being ignored, given the brush off or even being actively disliked but this was different. This was

Ford's family. He needed them to know how good they were together. *Right, no pressure.*

Ford picked the seat closest to his father and opposite his mother, leaving Reef to take the seat at the only other place set. Immediately after they sat, the same waitress who'd poured the wine laid the thick linen napkins over their laps. Ford's mother watched the lady like a hawk, scowling as she smiled at Ford. Ford's beaming smile back would have had Reef jealous if their hands weren't inter-linked under the table.

"Shall I run through the menu now, Sir? Madam?"

"Please." Dr. Wallace nodded.

"You will begin with a fillet of baked salmon served with a cucumber cream sauce and asparagus. Following that, lobster tail poached in buerre monté infused with butter, served on a bed of wilted baby spinach with baby red potatoes. Finally, for dessert, key lime pie served with double cream and candied lime shavings."

"Thank you. That will be all," Mrs. Wallace stated dismissing the young lady. Reef was mortified with her behavior and watched in sympathy as the waitress raced back into the kitchen, letting the swinging door whoosh closed behind her.

As soon as they were alone, Ford's father stopped toying with the stem of the wine glass and lounged in the wing-backed chair he sat in. Directing his glare at Ford, the clear disgust on his features shocked Reef. With brows lowered and his upper lip curled into a snarl, the self-righteous bastard made no effort to hide his disapproval. "Stratford, would you care to explain this nonsense to us? It's a rather ill-timed April Fool's joke."

Reef's gaze bounced to Ford. He mirrored his father's stance — relaxed in his chair, legs spread, looking completely indifferent. If it weren't for the tight grip he had on Reef's hand, Reef would have believed he was completely unaffected by his parents' reaction. "Oh, it's no joke, Father. Reef and I are dating."

"Assuming we accept that, Stratford, do you genuinely expect us to accept that he is good enough for you? He is clearly uncultured. Have you no regard for your future?"

Reef suddenly understood what it was like being a Ping-Pong ball, looking back and forth between Ford and his parents as they argued it out. Watching Mrs. Wallace sit perfectly upright with her hands clasped on her lap and her lips pursed as tight as a cat's asshole, disappointment washed over Reef. There was no hope they would be accepted in this household. Reef sympathized with Ford's reaction when Coach had left dinner. The crushing defeat stole his breath and made his heart hurt. Ultimately, Reef couldn't care less whether he had their approval but there was no way he'd stand between Ford and his family. Losing Ford was inevitable and it was going to destroy him.

The anger in Ford's voice surprised Reef. "Mother, I'm going to humor you just for a moment. Reef is one hell of—"

"Language, Stratford," his father shot back.

Ford glared at him before continuing, "Reef is the best kind of man. He risked his life to dig me out of an avalanche." Ford sat forward, no longer trying to hide his aggravation. Pointing at Reef he went on, his voice a deep growl as anger radiated from him. "He carried me for hours to get us to safety. He's brave and caring, he's loving and funny and has more talent in his little finger than I could ever hope to have."

Completely unperturbed by Ford's ire, his father looked unimpressed, shaking his head at Ford. "Yes, I heard about your unfortunate failure a few days ago. Stratford, I'm disappointed in you. Your diagnosis was sloppy and with the right care, your patient could have survived."

"Wait a minute," Reef interjected, horrified. Shifting in his seat to face Ford's father, he demanded, "What are you talking about?" Directing his question to Ford he asked, "Is he talking about the guy who died on the slope?" When Ford blinked his eyes closed and nodded, Reef's anger bubbled over. Slamming his glass down on the table, Reef stood, pointing down at Ford's father and shouted, "How dare you? How dare you criticize his effort to save that man. He did everything he could. He did everything right."

With an air of self-confidence he'd only seen on *James Bond*, Ford's father raised his eyebrows questioningly. "Did he? The man died, didn't he?"

"What, you've never had one of your patients die?" Reef bellowed as Ford grasped his hand tugging him back down into his seat. It took everything within Reef not to climb over the table and beat the man into a pulp.

Ford laughed bitterly, "Tell him Father. Tell him how you choose your patients based on their level of risk. You won't pick one up unless the operation is so straightforward you can practically guarantee they won't die on you. Your survival rate is second to none but it's because you take no risk. You let good people die because you won't accept them as a patient, not because you tried to help and failed."

"That's enough, Stratford," his father growled, showing the first chink in his emotions since they'd arrived. *So the man is human. He doesn't give a flying fuck about his son, only his job. Fucking bastard.* Reef's fists were curled so hard his knuckles were white. Damn, what he would give to have a minute alone with the good doctor so he could rearrange his face.

"So what is it that you do, Reef? Is that your birth

name? Reef?" Mrs. Wallace asked, without any attempt at hiding the venom in her voice.

Taking a deep breath in an attempting to let his anger simmer to a dull roar, Reef responded, "Yes it is, Ma'am. I'm a pro-snowboarder; a professional sportsperson. I ski on the world circuit."

"So you play for a living?"

"My job is wonderful, yes. But it's physically demanding too."

"How many world championships have you won?" this from Ford's father.

"None, Sir. I'm attempting to bring one home this year." Apparently that wasn't a good enough answer for Dr. Wallace who shook his head at Reef's comment.

Ford's voice broke Reef's stare-down with his father. "You've got it in the bag, sweet. You can't lose with the jumps you've been pulling off." A tingle shot through his bones and melted his heart at the warmth there. Ford curled his fingers around Reef's, his strong grip encouraging. Reef gave him a small smile. He could have hugged him in that moment but he wasn't sure how that would go down in front of Ford's parents. *Do I give a shit?*

"And your education? What do you have to fall back on when your sporting career is over?"

Way to make him feel like an underachiever. "Nothing, Sir. I haven't focused on that yet; I've dedicated myself to building up my skills as a snowboarder. My tour schedule is pretty grueling. I don't really have any time to study during the season and I tend to follow the snow to the southern hemisphere, training outside of the competition months. I have money saved, so when I finish I have enough to support myself and to get my college degree."

"Right."

"So what about children, Reef? How do you plan on giving my son offspring to carry on the family name?" *Fucking hell.* Reef's eyes widened at the bluntness of the line of questions during their interrogation.

"Mother, that's enough. When the time is right there are options for us to have children if we decide to but we're hardly there yet."

"Stratford, you're throwing your life away with this man. He's uneducated, clearly not from a respectable family — listen to his accent — and it's an embarrassment to your family name to be with a man. If you have to be gay, fine. Just don't bring it here. Find a nice lady who you can marry and keep a man on the side. What you do in private is nobody's business but you must maintain appearances."

"To whom, Mother?" Ford roared, surging to his feet and slamming his fist on the table knocking two wine glasses into each other. They shattered the instant they touched. The chair Ford sat on slid back along the polished floorboards so fast, it toppled over smashing awkwardly against the drywall. "What the fuck? Are you telling me to get married and cheat on my wife so I can fuck a man behind her back? What the fuck is wrong with you?"

"Stratford, sit down," his father ordered loud enough the waitress— who was half way through the swinging door from the kitchen— blanched, color draining from her face as she stopped mid-stride. Backing up, she left them to the worst conversation Reef had ever been involved in. At least if they had food in front of them they could eat. And not talk.

"I have no objection to you being gay, Stratford—" Dr. Wallace started.

"Pardon me?" his mother interrupted. She stopped

talking at Dr. Wallace's withering look, sinking back into her seat like a scolded child.

"As I said, I have no objection to you being gay, Stratford. It seems to be a trend more and more people are following. But I will not stand by and allow you to waste your life with *him*." Ford's father pointed at Reef disgust once again curling his lip. *Fucking prick.*

Ford's calmness surprised Reef. He'd be lying if he denied being fooled by the poker face Ford was forcing. But Reef knew him well enough that he could see the twitch in his temple, his slightly flared nostrils. "Father, this isn't some fashion trend I'm participating in to look cool. Reef is important to me and I'd appreciate it if you started to understand that."

"I'm sorry, this was a mistake," Reef spoke up as he stood with Ford. "You're right, I'm not good enough for him—"

"Reef, no." Ford replied, laying a hand on his arm to stop him.

"No, Ford. Let me speak." Turning back to his parents, he continued, "The truth is I *am* uneducated. I started as a pro before I'd even finished school. I'd be lucky to get into college with the marks I got in my final year. I don't come from a family that even fits in your society, never mind being respected in it. After my real parents decided I wasn't worth the trouble anymore, they left me in the hands of my high school football coach and his wife. He's king in the town I come from but no one even knows him outside of the high school roster. I'm not a winner, I'm not successful. I'm no society wife. But Ford is the best man I know. He makes me want to be a better man, makes me try to be better for him. We support each other in every way. He's everything to me. I may not be able to give him kids or fit into your world but I'll give him my all, every part of me."

Ford's father looked at him. Bored? Whatever it was, it was like a knife to Reef's heart. There really was no hope. He'd deluded himself into thinking they might eventually understand but he'd never see acceptance from them. Three out of four of their parents wanted nothing to do with him, with them. How would they survive this?

This time the doors swung open and the waitress marched inside, quickly placing plates in front of Dr. and Mrs. Wallace and moving around to Ford and Reef. The conversation ceased; a pregnant pause hovering in the air while the interruption ensued but as soon as the door swung shut, Ford's father started speaking again.

"Stratford, if you must try out being gay for a while there are plenty of men who are appropriate to your status as a Wallace and would make a better experiment than this man. If you do decide to go with this permanently, they would make far better husbands. Dr. Dennison is quite effeminate," Ford's father continued. "Maybe he's gay too. I'm not sure, but he could be. And Philip Butler, the lawyer. He's definitely gay. Much more suitable. He comes from a good family and he's a partner in a top law firm. Good looking too, I suppose if you like that thing."

Reef couldn't look at them anymore. He was way beyond wishing for a sinkhole to open up and swallow him. Bear attack might be good. Hell, even getting trampled by a moose would be better than this hell. It wasn't until Ford moved that Reef turned his attention to him. His man was livid: his face an angry red, his jaw clenched tight and hands fisted on the table top as he pushed back from it.

"You have some nerve speaking to me, to us, like this," he growled. Pointing between his parents, Reef watched as

Ford's tenuous hold on his temper frayed further. Reef's own emotions were bouncing between disappointment, anger, sadness, and fury. It took all his strength not to let rip again. "If I spoke to you, or one of your friends the way you have to Reef and me, I would have had the strap before I'd even finished the sentence. Since when did the level of disrespect you've shown a guest in this house become acceptable? I'm disgusted by you." Ford turned his back on his parents stepping away from the table.

"Stratford, we are your parents. You will not speak to us like that."

"You hypocritical fuckers," he spat, spinning on his heel and getting up in his father's personal space. "I can't speak to you like this but you'll disrespect my partner all you like? Not gonna fucking happen." As his father stood slowly, Ford took another step closer as if daring the doctor to give him a reason to knock him on his ass. "It's a damn good thing I never wanted into your life. I don't give a fuck who you think is a suitable husband or wife for me. It's my decision," Ford growled at his father, poking himself in the chest with his thumb before he pointed to Reef. "And I'm choosing Reef. Accept it or not, I don't give a fuck. I love him and I'm not giving him up. I don't want anyone else, some lame replacement who you deem worthy. He is good enough, more than worthy. He's mine and I'm his—" Ford's words sunk into Reef's brain as he continued screaming at his father. *"I love him."*

"Ford, hon," Reef said quietly as he cupped his man's arm. When Ford didn't react to Reef's touch and kept shouting at Dr. Wallace, Reef shook his arm and spoke louder. "Ford, stop shouting. Look at me."

Ford did and Reef cupped his face. "You do?"

"What?" Ford asked, confused.

"You love me?"

Ford gave him a sad smile. "Yeah, sweet, I do. With every part of me. I'm sorry I yelled it at them rather than telling you first." Reef pressed his forehead against Ford's before leaning in for a kiss. Fingers tangling in his hair, Reef pressed their mouths together again.

"Urgh, my appetite is ruined now. Get that woman in here to collect these." The arrogance in Ford's father's tone astounded Reef but right at that moment, he didn't give a shit that they were in the room.

"Should we get outta here, Reef?"

"Yeah, let's go." Joining their hands, Reef followed Ford as he stepped away from the table. "Wait, hon. I gotta duck into the kitchen."

"Yeah, great idea."

Pushing through the swinging door, Reef smiled at the waitress who was washing dishes as the chef worked madly away. "I'm so sorry that we're going to miss your cooking, but we're leaving. Supper smells amazing, though. Thank you for looking after us."

"Best of luck to you," the chef replied in a thick French accent. "I hope you are very happy together."

"Thank you," both Ford and Reef responded in unison. Ford squeezed his hand before nudging his shoulder. Warmth infused Reef's heart knowing he and Ford were solid, despite all the shit that had just gone down.

CHAPTER NINE

FORD UNLOCKED the SUV before he trapped Reef between his arms, pressing his back against the car. Bodies aligned, he leaned forward touching their lips together whisper-soft. Opening his mouth and licking along the seam of Reef's lips had his man responding in kind. Their tongues tangled as he captured Reef's moan. Bringing his hands to Reef's face, Ford gently cupped it as he poured everything into their connection.

Reef surprised him when he pulled back, putting a sliver of a gap between them. "I love you, Ford."

"You do?"

"Yeah, hon. I do."

"Tell me again, Reef."

"I love you." Ford watched his man as the smile lit up has face, his dimples giving him a boyish appeal on a sexy-as-sin man. He couldn't help smiling back. He'd found the love of his life and Reef felt the same. "Now, take me home, get me naked and make me come, Ford." That sexy smirk touched his lips and Ford fell even harder.

"I love you, too. So much."

· · ·

THANK Christ for quiet roads because Ford hadn't been able to keep his mouth off Reef's. Stopping at a red light he'd pulled Reef toward him and pashed his man straight through the signal changing twice. There'd been no honking horns or shouts of abuse to interrupt them.

"We'll never get home if you don't drive," Reef murmured against his lips. "And I really wanna get home."

"Me too," Ford moaned after Reef swiped his tongue into Ford's mouth gettin' frisky with him and letting his hands wander up under Ford's sweater.

CLOSING the door to the townhouse softly behind him, Ford grasped Reef's hands in his own. Standing in the middle of the little foyer, Ford smiled softly at Reef and pulled him in close. "I can't believe we're here, that we found each other. I've never been more grateful for a whiteout in my life."

Reef stepped closer coming into Ford's personal space, exactly where Ford wanted him. He wrapped his arms around his man, resting his hands at the small of Reef's back as Reef ran his own up his arms and tangled them in Ford's hair. Truth be told, he used to hate people playing with his hair but then Reef came along. His reaction to Reef's touch was visceral, turning his legs to jelly, his brain to mush and his cock to an iron rod.

With Reef's fingers wrapped in his curls, Ford closed his eyes and reveled in the touch which grounded him and at the same time, set him free.

"So am I. I thought I wanted to get away, to change my life. Turned out, I just needed to find you. Oh my God, could I be any sappier? See what you've done to me?" Reef laughed, playfully poking Ford in the chest. "Damn that was corny. True, but corny."

"So, better than a tropical island?"

"Yeah, but I've been thinking that we should do the island thing. You in a tight bathing suit? One of those little pairs that only just cover your ass. Fucking hot." Reef ran his hands down Ford's front, letting them trail away as he reached the waist of his jeans. Ford's cock jumped at the near contact.

"Dude, I'm a board shorts kinda guy. But you in pair of those tight underwear you wear, well that's fucking hot. I can picture you on a beach wearing nothing but those. Or maybe not even that." *Fuck yeah.* That thought had Ford's cock thickening in his jeans, hardening even more. He couldn't help his eyes from sliding closed and the soft moan that escaped him as Reef pressed their groins together. Reef's chuckle had him cracking one eye open.

"You like my underwear, do you?" Stepping back to put a sliver of distance between them Reef grinned wickedly, flashing those dimples again as he slowly pulled his sweater over his head revealing perfectly formed pecs and a set of washboard abs to die for. Low slung jeans cupped a package, which Ford knew from experience, could send him into orbit. He couldn't contain his growl as Reef adjusted himself and flicked open the top button of his fly.

Reef's head fell back and Ford barely resisted tasting the exposed skin near the pulse point. He reached out for Reef as his man whispered in barely more than a throaty moan, "Maybe for our honeymoon. We'll..." Reef's body went rigid and his head snapped up, his words trailing off. Wide eyed, panic radiated from him.

Confused at his abrupt halt in the conversation, Ford asked, "What, sweet cheeks? We'll what?"

Reef visibly swallowed, his Adams apple bobbing. It was ordinarily a sight that turned Ford on. Now it sent a twinge of panic through him.

"I just...I'm sorry, I know we spoke about getting married to a girl at the ranger's cabin but we've never spoken about *us* getting married. I assumed..." he trailed off again, no longer meeting Ford's gaze and shaking his head.

Marriage, kids; they weren't really something Ford had thought about. Until Reef.

Now he wanted it. All of it. And not his parents' fucked up version of marriage, but Coach and Momma Bear's kinda happiness. Ford smiled, stepping forward to eliminate the distance between them. Tipping Reef's face up, Ford brushed his lips over his man's. "Marrying you could be fun," he teased. "But in the meantime, a holiday together on an island sounds like paradise. Now, stop thinking so hard and get those jeans off. I'm suddenly ravenous."

Ford shivered as Reef slipped warm hands under his sweater and tugged the soft wool over his head. His T-shirt went too. Skin-to-skin, Ford joined their mouths together swiping his tongue over Reef's lower lip seeking entry and being rewarded immediately. They stumbled toward the bedroom, not pausing for air until they were both breathless. Ford let his hands explore all the pale skin before him.

When the back of Reef's knees hit the bed, Ford gave him a gentle shove and crawled over him, licking and nibbling his way up his abs and chest to his throat. Reef's muscles contracted under his touch, flexing and rippling as he squirmed at each press of his lips. Licking around one nipple and sucking the flat nubbin into his mouth, Ford bit down, applying just enough pressure to have Reef arching and crying out.

With one hand on the bed to support his weight, Ford used the other to rub Reef's erection through his jeans. Reef's scent filled his nostrils — an outdoorsy manly smell that always had his own cock standing on end — as he explored all that smooth warm skin with his mouth. Trailing his tongue over every ridge and valley, he took his time to love on his man, teasing and tempting him.

"More, Ford. I need more," Reef gasped.

Ford was only too happy to oblige. Popping the button fly on Reef's jeans, Ford tugged them down to reveal those sexy-as-sin black briefs Reef always wore. Pressing his lips against Reef's cloth covered shaft, he moaned. Heat and hardness met his mouth.

Nuzzling his man, Ford worked Reef's jeans down as far as he could without moving from his position. Climbing off the bed, he tugged Reef's jeans the rest of the way off. Ripping open his fly, he let his jeans drop to the floor and kicked both pairs aside. Reef had already stripped his remaining clothes so Ford did the same.

Completely naked, he returned to his place between Reef's bent legs and watched his man stroke himself. His eyes drifted closed as he gripped his cock tighter. His hips lifted off the bed with each tug. Ford followed suit, fisting his own shaft. Unable to resist the temptation before him, Ford leaned forward, licking a path up Reef's balls to the tip of his cock. Ford mouthed him as he cried out. Letting go of his own shaft, Ford pressed both hands on Reef's legs opening him further, exposing his taint.

He hadn't done it before, hadn't reciprocated the many times Reef had rimmed him. But that was going to change.

Ford had never wanted anything more in his life than to bliss Reef out.

Pushing his legs back further, Ford leaned down and licked a path along Reef's inner thigh toward the puckered ring tempting him. Reef's musky scent hit him as his tongue met soft skin. They moaned at the same time. Ford was addicted. Diving in, he lapped at Reef, circling and nipping at him until Reef was writhing below him.

"Oh God, Ford. Fuck me. Please. I need you inside me."

Ford tensed his tongue, pressing it into Reef, relaxing the muscle with his small intrusions. His man shuddered, moaning and gasping as Ford made love to him.

"Ford, please. I'm gonna come."

Ford pulled back, reaching for the lube and the condom sitting on the nightstand. He ripped it open and squeezed the tip, ready to roll it down his aching length.

"I'm clear, Ford. Come in me bare."

Ford stilled. Had he heard Reef right? Bare?

"It's okay, I get it if you don't want to." Reef closed his eyes and turned away from Ford.

Ford laid over him, pressing their bodies together. "Sweet cheeks, I want nothing more. But you don't know about me." Ford pressed kisses down his throat.

"I trust you. You said you hadn't gone bare with—"

"I'm clear, too. I got tested before I left Queenstown. Results were emailed to me."

"Make love to me, Ford. Nothing between us. Nothing but us."

No more words were needed. Ford lubed up his fingers and pressed them against Reef's hole. Loosening him more, he added a second then a third before pulling out.

"You ready for me, sweet?"

Reef nodded and Ford lubed up his cock, lying back

over Reef and lining himself up at his entry. Reef wrapped his legs around him and ran his fingertips along Ford's face. Taking a breath, Ford pushed forward breaching him as they stared at each other.

Resting their foreheads together, Ford withdrew a little and thrust deeper, slowly bottoming out. Tight, wet heat surrounded him and it took all Ford's strength not to come right then.

Strong fingers tangled in his hair as he sucked on Reef's throat, cradling his man's body in his arms. Moving slowly together, Ford breathed him in, tasted his salty skin, moaned as Reef found the spot on his back that sent shudders through Ford and had him pressing in harder.

Ford found himself on his back when Reef ran his foot down his leg, hooked it behind his knee and pushed. With Reef straddling him, Ford ran his hands up Reef's sides looking his fill as his man arched back. Reef rested his hands on Ford's uplifted knees and began moving.

Ford couldn't stop touching him, trailing his palms over every inch he could get his hands on, all the while being enveloped in heaven. Watching Reef use his powerful legs to lift and lower himself on Ford's shaft, riding him slowly, deeply was more than Ford could handle. Already skating the edge of an orgasm, he reached for Reef's dick. He needed him to be right there with him. Precum wet his fingers as Ford brushed the tip of Reef's cock. It dripped onto Ford's abs as he fisted him.

Sitting up in a crunch Ford touched his tongue against Reef's shaft as his man raised himself almost all the way off his cock. Urging Reef closer, he lifted his knees higher, pumping his hips up into Reef. He closed his mouth around the flared head of Reef's dick and laved his tongue over the slit. Massaging Reef's balls, he knew the moment Reef reached the point of no return. His ass clamped down around Ford's cock, his shaft pulsing in Ford's mouth. Reef shouted out as the first splash of cum hit Ford's mouth. Warm and salty, it coated his tongue, making him swallow. And it kept coming. Jet after jet releasing into him as Reef's movements stuttered.

Seeing his man so undone sent Ford to the edge too. He moaned long and loud as the hot fisted grip of Reef's channel overwhelmed him. Ford couldn't close his eyes, even though instinct told him to. His sight was locked on Reef, watching his man writhe above him and milk every drop of ecstasy out of their connection. He was Ford's drug of choice.

His aphrodisiac.

An addiction of the best kind.

The buzz at the base of his spine exploded outward and Ford's hips stuttered in their rhythm the same way Reef's had. His essence pumped into Reef joining them, marking them as one. Reef slumped forward catching himself on his elbows, pressing Ford down into the bed in exactly the place Ford wanted to be. Both of them breathing heavily, the world around them was slow to come back into focus. With jelly arms, Ford ran his hands up and down the smooth skin of Reef's damp back as Reef laid open mouthed kisses on the sensitive spot below his ear.

"Tell me again," Reef whispered.

"I love you." Ford nuzzled his temple, holding him tight. This man was his everything; being able to tell him that only made Ford fall harder. All the angst, all the anger and hurt his parents inflicted on them fled when he was wrapped in his man's arms. Kissing him softly, he added, "So much, Reef."

Reef hummed a sound of content, laying another line of

kisses down Ford's throat as he squeezed him tighter. Their bodies were pressed together, every inch joined; it was exactly what Ford needed in that moment. "I love you, too," Reef whispered into the crook of his neck, his warm breath sending shivers through Ford.

Ford's heart beat wildly, his and Reef's bodies plastered together all sweaty and sated, every limb like jelly. Rolling them, he slipped from the bed and on wobbly legs staggered to their attached bathroom. Waiting for the water to warm, he brushed his teeth and studied the familiar blue eyes in the mirror. They were so like his father's and yet wildly different too. Seeing his father in all his arrogant glory had reinforced the one thing Ford had been struggling with for years—he didn't want to belong in their world, wasn't going to turn into them. One thing Ford knew beyond any doubt was his future would revolve around love and laughter with Reef, not stuffy formal dinners and having to prove himself to angry parents. Slipping back in bed with cold toes and a warm washcloth, Ford ran the towel over Reef's smooth skin and tossed it aside, snuggling into his man. Spooning him, Ford intertwined their fingers and Reef squeezed tight as Ford kissed him. Warm, salty skin against his lips tempted him to taste a line down Reef's throat and shoulder before he laid his head down and breathed in his man.

"Night, hon." Reef yawned.

"Reef?"

"Hmm? Wassup?"

"Nothing, sweet. I... I'm sorry about tonight. About what they said."

"You don't need to apologize for them, Ford." Reef rolled over so they were face-to-face and cupped his cheek before moving to play with the curls at the nape of his neck. The love and comfort from Reef's warm hand against his skin had Ford sinking into the touch. "Never apologize for them."

Even in the dim light shining in from the lit corridor, Ford could see the seriousness in Reef's gaze, his adamancy that the hateful words his parents threw at them weren't going to come between them. Holding Reef close to him he whispered, "Have I told you lately I love you?"

"Yeah." Reef smiled, resting their foreheads together. "But I'm happy to hear it again." He pressed his lips to Ford's and hummed as their tongues tangled.

FORD LAY AWAKE LONG after Reef had fallen asleep wrapped around him. Looking up at the ceiling, he cradled Reef's head against his chest and ran his fingers gently up and down his spine. The weight of Reef's arm around his waist and the soft breaths ghosting along his skin were comforting but his mind was running at a million miles an hour. Unable to lie still anymore and not wanting to wake Reef up, Ford slipped out of bed and tugged on a pair of sweats. Padding down the corridor and into the combined family and dining room, Ford stoked the coals, adding a few logs and bringing the flames back to life. Warmth radiated from the fireplace quickly, chasing the chill from the night air. He boiled the kettle and dropped a chamomile tea bag into his mug, adding a squeeze of lemon once the tea had steeped a while.

Carrying the steaming liquid over to the window, Ford looked out at the towering mountains overhead. The white slopes reflected the moonlight in the clear sky. Days were getting shorter, nights longer and darker. He wondered whether the northern lights would be visible in the skies from Fernie. Craning his neck he looked up. Twinkling stars filled the inky sky, dotting the blanket of darkness with pinpricks of light.

It was beautiful. Silence surrounded him except for the crackle of the fire behind him. The glow of the snow on the mountaintop ahead was almost ethereal. Magical in a way. Virtually untouched. Pure. Ford wished he felt the same way. His father's words, hell his mother's words too, kept replaying in his mind. They made him uncomfortable, dirty even, knowing he was raised by two people who were so cold, so callus that they could only see how his being in love with Reef would harm the family name. Then Reef mentioned marriage and the wheels started turning there. *Would we hyphenate? Should I change my name?* That'd be one way to piss off the folks but was Ford giving up a part of himself that, although different to the way his parents saw him, was still him, his identity? *Would Reef even care?*

And then there was the problem of Coach. Reef had spoken with Momma Bear since they'd gone there for supper but it had been strained. When he hung up any other time he'd be smiling, happy. She was that sort of person for Reef — she lifted his spirits. But the conversation was awkward now and he was more stressed than when he'd been fretting over whether he should call. Coach still hadn't given her any indication he wanted to restart the dialogue between them and that was especially hard on Reef. Ford wouldn't give him up for the world but what about for Reef's family?

Leaning his head on the cold glass, he looked through the second pane to the street below. A couple staggered back home after a night out. A car drove slowly through the village. He could see a light from down the street where the bar was located, no doubt packed to capacity now the inn was closed for repairs. He sighed and closed his eyes.

"That's a heavy sound from someone who managed to make me blow like Mount St. Helens a few hours ago." Reef spoke from behind him, startling Ford. The cooling tea spilled from the mug onto Ford's hands.

"Oh shit, are you okay?" A very naked Reef rushed over and wiped the liquid off Ford's hands with his own.

"It's not hot anymore, sweet cheeks. Why are you up?"

Stroking a hand down Ford's back he replied, "I lost my pillow and your side of the bed got cold. Are you okay?"

"Can't shut down my mind but it's alright. You should go back to bed. You've got your first day back at training tomorrow."

"It's just some film in the morning and a light workout in the afternoon. Mace doesn't want to push me too hard yet. He's paranoid about the smoke." Ford leaned into the touch when Reef gently squeezed his hip, "Come on, talk to me, please."

"Yeah. Yeah, okay." Reef led them to the long sofa and sat down in the corner, one leg up against the chair back, the other spread wide and motioned for Ford to sit between them. Spread like that, Reef was a hell of a sight but it wasn't what either of them needed at that moment. Ford shook out the neatly folded blanket and wrapped it around Reef's shoulders.

"Always looking after me," Reef teased.

"Always." Ford smiled as he sat down and leaned back against Reef's warm chest. Strong arms wrapped around his shoulders, covering them both in the soft blanket and Reef's prickly stubble rubbed gently against his temple. It was familiar, comforting. He'd never in a million years have believed he'd be sitting wrapped in a man's arms, never mind this man, who he'd been a fan of for years.

"You ever been ashamed of where you came from?"

Ford asked rhetorically. He knew Reef's relationship with his real parents wasn't great. Thanks to them, Reef had a few abandonment issues. Thankfully, they'd managed to work through them so far without Ford screwing things up too badly and making those insecurities worse. And Momma Bear and Coach were the best pseudo parents he could have ended up with; far better than Ford's real parents.

Without giving Reef a chance to answer he continued. "They really let me down tonight. I'm disgusted that their outlook on life is so jaded by status and money that they look at a family as a social symbol. Whatever happened to unconditional love? Hell, do they even know what love is? Why did they even have me? Was it just because it was the done thing? Jesus, I can't even comprehend that."

Holding him tight, Reef asked, "How come you turned out so different? Don't get me wrong, I'm glad you are, but how did you shield yourself from them?"

"I dunno. I just hated all the pomp and ceremony that they live for. Like the caterer tonight. Seriously, two people to serve them? I'm surprised Mother answered the door and didn't send that poor lady she had waiting on them to do it. Urgh. I hated the conversations at school about whose father had the most successful business and drove the most expensive car. And they only got worse the older the kids got. I just wanted to help people. Suppose it was good that medicine fit nicely in my father's plans but I wasn't in it for the status. I genuinely wanted to make a difference. Either way, I'm just glad I managed to break free young enough not to have turned out like them."

"Yeah, I get it," Reef replied squeezing him tighter, humming when Ford skated his palm up Reef's leg. Just feeling his solidness underneath Ford, the bulk of his lean body, the masculinity of defined muscles grounded Ford, brought him home.

"I just wanted them to hear me out, ya know? To let the fact that I'm happy make them happy for me. For us. But apparently it's irrelevant unless you're socially acceptable to them." Even Ford heard the hopelessness in his voice. Ultimately he didn't care what his parents' thought but being faced with the reality of their rejection was hard. Reef dropped a soft kiss against Ford's temple. That small gesture was more comfort than he could ever remember receiving from either of his parents. In some ways it hurt even more but it also made him love his man harder.

"Do you want to talk to them more about it?"

"Not right now. I'm too bloody pissed off at them."

"It's two in the morning. It wasn't gonna be now." Reef laughed.

"Smart ass." Ford smiled as he playfully pinched the soft skin on the inside of Reef's thigh.

"I don't know if I do wanna speak with them again. If we weren't related, I'd have nothing to do with them." Ford took a deep breath and exhaled slowly, trying to force the anger toward his parents to abate. It didn't work until Reef started massaging his shoulders.

"But blood is pretty thick."

Ford turned, looking at Reef and shook his head. "Not if it'll hurt you." The comfortable silence lingered between them for a moment while they gazed at each other. So much love in Reef's warm browns. He could get lost in those eyes, often did. Reef's hand at the back of Ford's head drawing him close for a kiss had his eyes sliding closed as their lips slowly melded together. Eventually breaking apart, Ford rested his head on Reef's shoulder once more and continued their conversation,

"What about you, sweet cheeks? You gonna try Coach again?"

"Yeah, tomorrow. I'm gonna call him in the morning and see if he'll meet me for a coffee after my workout. I need to know one way or another, even if it's that he doesn't want anything to do with me."

"What happens if he says that?" Ford asked, closing his eyes and steeling himself for the answer.

"It'll suck, but if he can't accept us then I can't ask more of him." The tension drained out of Ford so quickly he physically slumped against Reef. The rumble in Reef's chest made him look up at his man smiling sadly at him. "I won't hurt you either, bunnykins."

"Oh fuck, that name." Ford laughed, shaking his head. Reaching up to cup Reef's cheek he whispered, "I love you, sweet," against his lips before laying a soft kiss against them.

"Love you too, hon."

Sighing contentedly, Ford laid his head back against Reef's shoulder, loving the strength of the embrace that cradled him so adoringly.

Ford was at peace; happy, despite the ugliness of his parents. Life, fate could throw whatever the fuck it liked at them. He and Reef were solid. A self-satisfied smirk crossed his lips. He'd manned up and said those three little words and fuck it felt good.

CHAPTER TEN

THE WORKOUT WAS GOOD, Reef was pumped after getting back into it. Mason had trained with him too, both of them building up a hell of a sweat in the lodge's gym. They were walking back to their adjacent townhouses when a black Range Rover pulled up to the curb. Reef looked twice but didn't slow his steps toward the front door.

"See ya, man. Good luck with Coach this afternoon. Call me, yeah?"

"Thanks, Mace. I will." Fist bumping his trainer, Reef pulled out his key to the front door. His cell beeped with a text as he walked inside, kicking the door closed behind him. Swiping his finger across the screen, Reef checked the display, smiling when Ford's name popped up.

I've been summoned for a meeting with Mother. Sorry, sweet, I'll be a little late getting back this afternoon.

Reef headed straight for the shower and started the water running letting it heat while he stripped off his sweats and underwear. The room had already started to steam as he stepped under the spray.

Reef showered quickly, the hot water soothing his tired

muscles. Sighing contentedly when he was clean, Reef turned off the water and stepped out wrapping a towel around his waist. Padding out of the attached bathroom into their bedroom, Reef's stomach protested loudly in hunger. Looking at the clock on his cell, he figured he had time to head over and grab a bite to eat before meeting Coach. Nerves fluttered in his belly in anticipation of their meeting. He didn't want to lose Coach and Momma Bear. The two of them meant the world to him but if Coach couldn't accept his being with Ford... well, he'd walk away from them before he gave up his man.

Slipping his heavy coat back on, Reef opened the front door to a blast of cold air. Reaching back inside to snatch his beanie off the coat rack, he pulled it down over his ears and spun around only to nearly walk into Ford's father.

"Ford is meeting with your wife, you're in the wrong spot if you wanna see him." Reef's tone was belligerent but he made no effort to hide it. Trying to push past him he stiffened, muscles tensing when Ford's father held his arm out blocking his path. Reef was on the defense — he trusted Ford's father as far as he could throw the man.

"It was actually you whom I wanted to see."

"I have nothing to say to you, Dr. Wallace."

"But I have something to speak with you about."

"Fine." Reef shrugged, hoping he could pull off half the poker face Ford could. Hearing Ford's father say he needed to speak with Reef had butterflies raging. Hope reared its head that things might actually work out. He wanted to hate the man but he couldn't bring himself to if there was any chance they could get past their differences especially if Ford's mother was trying to mend their relationship.

"I'm going out for lunch. You can follow me if you'd like."

"Thank you." Ford's father motioned to the Range Rover parked on the street. *He's the person who pulled up?*

"No thanks, I'll walk. It's only around the corner." Attempting to extend an olive branch to Dr. Wallace he added, "Feel free to walk with me if you like."

"Please," he motioned, holding out his hand for Reef to lead the way.

They began the trudge up the street. Hands in his pockets and head down, Reef braced against the cold wind buffeting them. The chill in the air was bone deep. *Or maybe it's just the company?* The silence between them was uncomfortable, awkward. Reef caved and looked across the sidewalk toward his boyfriend's father. The disdain in the other man's expression was palpable. Lips pursed with a scowl on his face aimed at Reef, it looked as if he wanted to squash him like a bug then scrape him off the bottom of his shoe. Reef sighed as hope quickly faded. It was gonna be a long-assed lunch. Dealing with Dr. Wallace and meeting Coach in the same afternoon, Reef hoped one of the meetings would go smoothly.

Pushing open the door to the lodge's grill, Reef entered and walked straight to his favorite booth. If nothing else at least their food would be good and the place was always vibin'. Groups of people high on life and the adrenaline buzz from a hella good mountain would hang here and it always made for a good time. It had drawn him in the first time he'd eaten at the restaurant years ago and he always returned. Set up as a retro 1950s ski lodge, the grill had style – a combination of Prince and *The Fonz* in a white fur coat. With old school service and great burgers and shakes he and Ford had eaten supper there a few days earlier, but no matter, the food was worth going back for a second time in a week.

Sitting down opposite him, Ford's father looked around the casual restaurant; his scowl remaining firmly in place.

"What can I do for you, Dr. Wallace?"

Before he could answer, Monique the owner's daughter, placed some menus on the table. "Hey gorgeous, can I just get my usual please?"

"Sure, Reef. Coming right up." Turning to Ford's father, she asked, "Can I get you anything, Sir?"

"No, I won't be eating."

"Sure, okay. Reef, I'll be back in a minute with your shake."

Reef looked at the doctor expectantly, waiting for the proverbial bucket of ice to be dropped on his mood. Outwardly, Reef was calm and collected but his insides were doing backflips, free-falls and hard landings all at the same time. He'd mastered hiding his nerves during competitions but he'd never been overly successful hiding his emotions off the mountain. Trying to do it in the face of a man who literally had the power and resources to make his life a misery was hell.

Clasping his hands and resting his forearms on the table in a pose Reef imagined the doctor would often use with his errant patients, Ford's father began speaking, "I'm going to cut to the chase. I don't want you seeing my son anymore."

Reef was momentarily stunned. Mouth hanging open and eyebrows no doubt arched so high they'd disappeared under his hairline, he took a moment to catch himself. Sitting up straighter and mirroring the doctor's pose, Reef replied forcefully, "Not gonna happen. Ford and I aren't breaking up because you don't like me."

"Ford has a bright future. All he has to do is accept he is entitled to it. His career choice leaves a lot to be desired but many in our circles will overlook the blue-collar nature of his work if he returns to the family and takes his place in our society. In order to do that, he must have someone beside him who will fit in appropriately. He must be able to continue his family's legacy and maintain his status."

Reef couldn't help the disbelieving laugh that erupted from him. "Are you serious?" He leaned back in the seat and shook his head. "Un-freaking-believab—"

The words died on Reef's tongue with the venom in Dr. Wallace's stare down. "I am deadly serious. You are not the right person for Stratford. You aren't even in the right ballpark, as you Americans would say. I can get past your gender. As I said last night, it seems to be something people are experimenting with. But your background will never be satisfactory." He counted Reef's faults off on his fingers as he spoke. "Your nationality is hardly ideal, but at least you're white," he conceded. "Your heritage is unacceptable. You're uneducated, uncultured and uncouth. I will not stand by and watch my son throw away his life with someone like you. *You* are undeserving."

Reef held his head up high knowing the insults were thrown by a man who was less sure of his place in Ford's life than Reef. Taking strength from that, Reef infused his voice with as much arrogance as Dr. Wallace's held. "Your son doesn't think that. I think his opinion matters way more than yours."

"My son doesn't know what's good for him. It's my job as his father to direct his future—"

"No, it's your job as a father to support him," Reef interrupted a lot louder than he'd intended. Leaning forward over the top of the table, Reef lowered his voice but kept the steel in his tone as he continued, "*You* have failed miserably at that. He's an adult. He doesn't need you to hover over him and tell him what he's allowed to do and isn't. What he *does* need is a little support. You knew about the man dying up on the slope. Instead of criticizing him, a little sympathy would have gone a long way. You know how fragile life is. You literally hold peoples' hearts in your hands. Yet you feel it's appropriate to diss your son when he tried his damnedest to save a man."

"He could have saved him if he was carrying the right equipment and diagnosed him properly," Ford's father replied mulishly.

"He's not working as a paramedic. He can't carry his bag. But if you bothered to listen to his news you would know that already, wouldn't you?" he asked rhetorically. Dr. Wallace knew Ford wasn't working as mountain rescue. He'd ripped his son a new one when he found out Ford had accepted a demotion in order to— as his father put it —get some pussy. Thinking of that Reef barely resisted the smirk from forming. Ford was doing it for ass, definitely not pussy.

Pointing at Reef, Dr. Wallace spat back, "My son would not have even been on that slope if he didn't chase you across the world." Jabbing his finger in Reef's direction again, he hissed, "This is on *you*."

Reef shook his head sadly. The fact that Ford's father didn't understand what he was doing disappointed but didn't surprise him either. "See, that's the difference between us. Instead of laying blame, I was there for him. He cried on *my* shoulder. *I* held him that night. Wake up to yourself. You're going to lose him if you don't change."

"No, I'm not. You're going to get up and walk out of his life. You're going to take the check for ten thousand dollars I have in my jacket and walk away. And you're never going to look back." Reef stilled and stared at him. *Did I hear right? Ford's father is trying to bribe me?*

It was surreal watching the good doctor reach into his

pocket and withdraw a check made out to cash for, yep, ten thousand dollars. He slid it slowly across the table so it lay in front of Reef.

Reef reared back in horror, plastering himself back against the seat to distance himself from the poison pill to his and Ford's relationship. "I'm not taking that. I'm not even going to touch it. Fucking hell, do you think that's all your son is worth?" Anger now infused his tone, Reef seeing red at the doctor's arrogance. "You're trying to buy him?" *Fucking sonofabitch.*

Dr. Wallace returned Reef's horror with a look of self-righteousness that was like a struck match kissing gasoline. Reef's fists clenched and he ground his teeth together daring Ford's father to keep speaking.

"No, I'm trying to save him. What do you want? Ten thousand was a starting point. I'm prepared to negotiate. Name your figure to walk away."

Shaking with barely contained rage, Reef ground out the words. "There isn't enough money in the world to make me turn my back on him you piece of shit. How dare you." He was gonna punch the bastard. Knock him flat on his ass and enjoy every second of it.

"Twenty thousand."

Smashing his clenched fists on the table and sending the butter knife clattering onto the floor, Reef lurched up menacingly hovering over Ford's father. Losing control of the rage bubbling within Reef like lava in a volcano, he shouted out, getting the attention of every diner in the grill. "You need to leave. Right. Fucking. Now."

"Not enough? Fine—"

"Did you know your son — the man who is a part of you — was hit by an avalanche a few months ago? Did he tell you how I dug him out? How I carried him for hours so I could get him back to safety?" Seeing the surprised widening of Dr. Wallace's eyes Reef continued, "At that moment I would have given anything to save him. I would have sold my soul to the devil himself to save him. When he opened his eyes, I knew. When I saw him walk off the plane at Calgary, I knew. When he ran into a burning building to get me out thinking I was still in there, I knew. When I open my eyes every damn morning, I know. I love him. He loves me. Nothing you do will *ever* change that. I will *never* walk away from him."

"Fifty thousand." Reef stared at him. Stone cold hatred pulsed through him. The doctor didn't flinch as Reef stared him down. "Come on, boy, you have a price. Name it and you'll get what you want."

Reef stepped out from the booth and pointed toward the door. The anger, which boiled through his veins, took every ounce of strength and restraint within Reef to stop from reaching out and grabbing Ford's father around the throat. Pounding the man into a bloody pulp on the linoleum floor of the grill would have felt really good right at that moment. "You need to close that fucking mouth of yours, and you need to leave. I never want to see you again, you hear me? Keep the fuck away from Ford, too."

Lounging in the booth seemingly unaffected by Reef's rage, those fucking clasped hands in his lap, Dr. Wallace responded mildly. "Calm down and let's talk about this like adults. There's no need to use language like that."

"Why, because it might offend your delicate ears? Fuck off."

Pulling a pen out of the pocket of his expensive blazer, Ford's father uncapped it and smiled coldly. "Everything in life is a negotiation, boy. Name your price and we'll go from there."

"Let's not calm down," growled a familiar deep voice. Coach. "My son has asked you to leave and you will do that right now or I will remove you."

The doctor's eyes flicked away from Reef's and met Coach's glare. At five foot eleven Coach wasn't tall, but he was broad-shouldered and still carried himself like the military veteran he was. Back ramrod straight and a booming voice, he commanded an audience everywhere he went. That audience's respect soon followed and he was worthy of it. He was a good man, a strong man who stood up for those he loved, who didn't mess around with pretenses or tiptoeing around the hard issues. Coach was the man who'd taught Reef what having a family meant, who showed him what the love of a father was really like. Not like this piece of shit in front of him. He wouldn't even spit on him if he were on fire.

"She cheated on you. In case you hadn't figured it out, your woman cheated on you." The doctor's smugness infuriated Reef but he wouldn't bite. He wouldn't lower himself to this prick's standards. Truth be told, Reef didn't feel like spending a night in the lockup facing assault charges. And after he got started by breaking this bastard's nose, he would definitely be arrested. Coach, however, had no such hesitation. Gripping the doctor hard around his bicep, he dragged him out from the booth and kept walking straight out the doors of the grill. It took a second for Reef to process what was happening but when he did, he scrambled behind them, sprinting out of the restaurant.

Both hands fisted in the man's shirt, Coach dragged the doctor's face down to his own height. Reef didn't hear the words that were spoken as he ran toward the door but he saw the look on Dr. Wallace's face as realization dawned. He knew he was about to get a beating. Coach would never stand for his beautiful wife's reputation being sullied. But Reef wasn't gonna watch Coach be carted off either.

As he slid to a halt next to Coach on the icy surface of the pavement, he placed a gentle hand on his arm. Reef could feel the tension and strength simmering along Coach's strong arms. "Dad," he spoke quietly, belying the anger that colored his own vision red. "Let him go. Ford and I won't be hearing from him again." Turning to stare down Ford's father he added, "Will we?" Reef's words may have been framed as a question, but there was no doubt in how he expected the doctor to answer. His tone was clipped, hard.

When Dr. Wallace didn't answer, Reef stepped closer. "Get this in that thick fuckin' skull of yours. You will not come near me again. You will not contact me again. You will never offer me anything to keep me away from Ford again. If Ford decides he wants nothing to do with you when he finds out what you've done— and believe me, he will —you will not contact him or go near him again either. But right now, your first priority is getting you and your wife on a plane to fly your snobby, not worth a piece of shit asses away from me and my man. Got it?"

Chin up defiantly, Ford's father stared at Reef until the fight drained out of him. "Yes, fine," he sighed.

Coach pushed him away as he let go of the doctor's coat. "Come on, Dad. Let's get a coffee," Reef spoke encouragingly.

The older man looked at Reef with glassy eyes filled with emotion. "I'd like that, son."

Throwing an arm around Coach's shoulders, they walked inside together. This time the aroma of fresh coffee and mouthwatering food hit him and his stomach growled appreciatively. They sat at the same booth Reef had sat at earlier, but this time the person sitting opposite him warmed his heart.

"I'm sorry, Reef. I was such a fool—"

"Dad, stop. There's no need. I get that you were uncomfortable." Reef reached out and patted his forearm.

"Is that what you thought? God, I'm even more of an idiot. I wasn't uncomfortable. I was... disappointed."

Reef's heart slammed against his chest. The pain from that statement was physical. Reef's hand automatically went to his chest to try to stop the sharp slicing sensation as he gasped for breath.

"Shit. I'm screwing this up again. I wasn't disappointed in you, Reef. You made me incredibly proud. You still do. You're so brave. I was disappointed because I was worried you were giving up your dreams. I've always known that you wanted to settle down and have a family. It wasn't lost on me that you are your parents' son, constantly on the move and never planting roots in one spot. But I knew when you found the right lady, you'd stop being a nomad in a heartbeat if it meant having the home you'd always dreamed of. Seeing you with Ford made me think that your dream would never come true; you'd never have the home, never have the children you so desperately want. I couldn't let you see how broken up I was for you when you were so happy. It hurt me to think that you were settling. I didn't want you to get hurt."

Reef nodded and Coach continued, "But then I realized you weren't settling if you love him. Momma Bear told me how hurt you were when Ford tried to step away to save our relationship. She also told me how much stronger you were together. That was of course after she kicked my ass for being an idiot." Coach laughed sadly. "I never want you to have to choose between your soul mate and your family.

You deserve better than that, Reef. I'm sorry I hurt you." Coach reached out placing a hand over Reef's.

"So, you're okay with Ford and I being together?"

"Do you love him?"

"Yeah," Reef nodded.

"And he loves you?"

"He does."

"You're happy together?"

Thinking about how ridiculously gooey and sweet the feels were when Ford was around him, Reef smiled shyly. "We are."

Coach smiled in response and the sight melted any worries Reef still carried. Grasping Coach's callused hand firmly, he took solace in the strength of the familiar grip. "Then yes, I'm more than okay with you two being together. How couldn't I be? I didn't lose non-existent grandchildren, I gained a second son. I always wanted two boys of my own."

Reef laughed, a carefree sound after the stress of the meeting with Ford's father. "You realize we probably won't play much football together? Ford's British, he plays soccer or rugby or whatever the hell it is they play over there."

"Who needs football when I can cheer you on to winning a world championship?"

"I love you, Dad." Reef smiled broadly and squeezed Coach's hand once more. "Thanks for supporting us. I think we're gonna need it after we sort through this shit-storm with Ford's parents."

"I only caught 'fifty thousand'. Tell me it wasn't what it sounded like."

"It was Ford's dickhead father offering me fifty thousand dollars to walk away from him. The prick actually tried to pay me off." Reef shook his head, all joviality gone from his expression.

"Where's Ford? I think you need to talk to him about it."

"Me too. He's with his mother." Reef winced, scared of the damage her words could inflict on Ford. He needed to call him. He needed to hear his voice. "Um, I—"

"Call him, Reef. I'll give you some privacy while I put our orders in."

Reef nodded, palming his cell while Coach stood and walked away. Bringing up his number, Reef dialed and waited for Ford to pick up, but the only voice he heard was Ford's recorded one asking him to leave a message.

"Call me, Ford. Please, hon. I need to talk to you." Pausing for a moment, realizing what the message sounded like, he added, "I love you. Bye."

CHAPTER ELEVEN

"Hello, Mother," Ford sighed into the phone as he gazed out over the mountain. He hated speaking with her while up there, hated the thought that she could somehow tarnish the untouched beauty of the white peaks behind him and the pristine slope before him with her words. Snow had fallen at dawn, not much, but enough that the previous day's tracks were covered. Only a few skiers had been out in his section of the bowl that morning. Most were in the lodge avoiding the bitterly-cold wind whipping up the slope. The wind didn't deter Ford from the virgin mountain laid out before him, tempting him to worship at the altar of the snow gods.

"Stratford, I'm so glad you picked up." Her voice was sweet, almost sickly so. After his parents' performance at dinner the night before, Ford wanted nothing to do with her but apparently that wish was going unfulfilled.

"You rang four times in a row. I figured you weren't gonna leave me alone until I answered you." The two skiers coming off the main ski lift caught Ford's attention and his gaze followed them as they carved through the snow, tossing up powder with every turn cutting back and forth.

"I'd like to discuss last night with you. Meet me at the Country Club in an hour, please?"

"That's not convenient, Mother. I don't get off shift for another hour and Reef and I have plans this afternoon."

"Your father and I are only here for a limited time before he needs to get back to London. Please make the effort."

"Fine," he sighed. "I can make a little time, but only a half-hour."

"Thank you."

"And I'm not going to the Country Club. You'll need to come up the mountain and meet me at the coffee shop in the lodge. I can meet you for coffee there in just over an hour."

Ford's mother sighed audibly through the phone. This was something she did often; her sighs conveying her disappointment with Ford's complete inability to co-operate with her more than reasonable requests, or as Ford liked to put it — he wasn't her little bitch. "Is it suitable?"

"What, do you mean is it suitable for someone as stuck up as you? If that's what you mean, no it's not, but if you want to see me, you'll come there."

"Don't use that kind of language with me, Stratford," she snapped. "Your upbringing was better than that."

"Whatever, Mother. I'm working. I'll see you when I get off." He hung up his cell before she could continue her diatribe, quickly typing out a message to Reef letting him know he'd have to change their plans:

I've been summoned for a meeting with Mother. Sorry, sweet, I'll be a little late getting back this afternoon.

Even thinking about his man made him smile. Falling

asleep on the sofa together after their early morning chat left both of them with creaky muscles but he wouldn't have changed it for the world. Not even the thought of dealing with his mother dimmed his smile.

———

FORD PUSHED through the door to the lodge's coffee shop, stripping off his coat as he went. The smell of freshly ground-roasted beans hit him and instantly he was reminded of Reef. This was his favorite place to get coffee in town. Ford had surprised him a few days earlier running out to pick up a steaming cup first thing in the morning while his man was still lazing about in bed. He'd been thanked in the best way possible. Repeatedly.

His mother's perfect hair was the first thing Ford spotted as he ambled across the warm shop. He gave the cute barista, Johnnie, a two-fingered wave as he dodged a few chairs and sat down opposite the woman who'd summoned him. "Hello, Mother."

"Oh, Stratford, how wonderful to see you."

"You didn't think so last night. In fact, you were down-right rude."

Their conversation was interrupted by the waitress. Ford jumped in to order with a smile. "Hi, love, one cup of English Breakfast tea, one Earl Grey, and a scone with strawberry jelly and cream." Turning to his mother he added, "Mother, scone?"

"Yes please, Stratford."

"Make that two scones with jelly and cream."

"No problem, Ford, coming right up."

His mother looked at him confused. "You know her?"

"Sure, I come in here often with Reef."

His mother was never one to get sidetracked for too long, efficiently bringing it back to the topic she clearly wanted to discuss. "You have to understand that your father and I were shocked. We never expected you to announce you had turned gay and especially not for someone so... different to you."

"Mother," Ford warned.

She toyed with the white paper napkin laid out on the table, looking the most vulnerable he'd ever seen her. "Stratford, you don't realize this, but I understand love. Your father and I do love each other. Our relationship isn't perfect, and sometimes we both make comments that are regrettable about our views on marriage — take last night for example, the suggestion I made was... unfortunate—"

"What, the one where you suggested I live a lie and cheat on my society wife so I can get my rocks off with a man?" Ford asked pointedly, sitting with his arms crossed over his chest, eyebrows arched up high as he leaned back in the armchair waiting for his mother to bite back at his smartass response.

"Stratford, let me finish," she replied, not taking the bait. "Ultimately your father and I love each other. We want that for you."

"Reef *is* that for me."

"I don't think he is. I think you're both convinced of that but it's not what you truly want." She shook her head. Ford looked at the woman before him. This was the most frank conversation they'd ever had, but Ford was still wary. Call him cynical, but his mother always operated with an agenda in mind. Was her love for him finally it? Or was there something else he couldn't yet see?

"How would you know what I want, Mother? You've never bothered to ask. Your assumptions about my future are based on what you and Father believe I should want. I'm not gonna give Reef up. It's not gonna happen."

"I'm not asking you to, Stratford. You were right, you're an adult and can make your own decisions. Understand, however, that your father and I will be there for you when this relationship goes pear-shaped." And there it was. His mother was so confident his and Reef's relationship was destined to fail that she figured she'd get what she wanted in the long-term.

Ford shook his head and shifted in his seat, barely resisting the urge to end the conversation once and for all by walking out on her. "So, you'll humor me until Reef and I call it quits, then you'll say 'I told you so'?"

His mother's words were caring; maybe he was wrong about his earlier assumption. "No, Stratford. But when it doesn't work out, I'll be here for you. To talk to, to be a shoulder to cry on — whatever you need." She reached across the table holding out her hand, palm up, waiting for him to take it. Ford eyed it like it carried a contagion and made no move to grasp her hand.

"Why do you say 'when' it won't work out?" he asked, unable to mask the vulnerability in his question.

"Because you want children, Stratford," she answered matter-of-factly. "You want a beautiful wife to come home to, who you can carry on your arm and be proud of. You don't want a man. One day you *will* wake up and under-stand that."

"And no doubt you'd be thinking 'I told you so'," Ford muttered under his breath.

"Stratford," his mother issued the warning this time and pulled back her hand. *Ah, there she is.* The cold stare she had pinned on him was the look of the mother he knew well.

"No, Mother. I've heard enough," Ford replied, pushing the small armchair back as he stood. "I'm in love with Reef. You say you understand love, well understand this. Really listen to what I'm saying. *I'm not giving him up.* I'm not going to get sick of him. I'm not going to wake up wondering why I married him not a Barbie doll that can hang off me and suck at my will to live. You might think you know what's best for me, but you don't. And seriously, saying you're there for me as a shoulder to cry on? My ass."

"Stratford," his mother gasped, exaggerating her shock by placing a hand over her mouth.

"I've heard enough, Mother. I appreciate you trying to fix what you and Father broke last night—if that's what you were really trying to do—but you've got a long way to go. Accepting Reef as a permanent fixture in my life will be a good start. You'll need to apologize to him, too. Until you're prepared to do both, don't bother calling me." Ford turned on his heel and strode away, only to have his mother call out desperately.

"Stratford, we don't want to lose you."

Ford turned and looked at the woman standing before him. She might as well have been a stranger rather than the woman who gave him life. She reached out to him, her body language begging him to return to her. Ford didn't move, knowing the only way he and Reef had a chance at winning their acceptance was to hold strong. "You know what you need to do then. It's as simple as that, Mother."

The waitress delivered a tray to the table and began unloading the cups, saucers and pots of tea. "Love, can I get mine to go, please. And I'll get a cookie and a coffee for Reef too, if you can."

"Sure, Ford. Ma'am, would you like yours to go, too?"

"No, thank you. I will take mine here."

Waiting at the counter, Ford glanced at his cell. *Shit, it's flat.* Reef was supposed to meet Coach that afternoon; they were probably talking things through in one of the other cafes or restaurants close by— it wasn't like there were many to choose from on the mountain. Ford hoped it was going well, better than his own conversation at least. *Am I being too harsh? She's making an effort. No, she needs to understand.* He steeled his resolve ready to walk away from his mother once and for all when his father strode past him, ignoring Ford altogether. He looked... rattled. And pissed off.

Ready to throttle someone in fact.

Oh fuck, what had he done?

As Johnnie handed him the tray with his steaming tea, Reef's coffee and the two takeaway bags of sweets, Ford smiled at the man but he didn't feel it.

"Enjoy, Ford." Nodding, he took the paper bags and hesitated only for a moment. His parents were having one of those whispered arguments, but it didn't look like they were angry with each other. That made the sinking feeling in Ford's gut worse. Reef. He needed to find Reef. Where would he be? He couldn't remember Reef saying where he was meeting Coach, but there was one way to find out.

Ford burst out of the coffee shop's front doors and looked down the street. Ski gear, souvenirs, hotel and a bar on the left hand side. On the right was their favorite burger place, another bar, the fire-damaged inn, and a second coffee shop. If he knew his man, he'd be hungry, wanting lunch after his workout. Burgers. Ford smiled, and this time it was real.

Grateful for the plastic covers over the hot cups in his hands, Ford jogged down the street to the burger place, dodging the skiers milling around the sidewalk and trying not to slip on the icy surface. Entering the 50s diner with a splash of disco, he spotted Reef instantly, a worried expression on his face as he palmed his cell. He was nodding at something Coach was saying. Ford stepped quickly toward them, accidentally kicking a chair as he moved. Reef's eyes met his an instant later. The relief washing over him visible; the tight lines around his eyes and his furrowed brow disappearing, replaced with a smile that lit up the room.

And those dimples? Swoon.

He could relate to those tweens who went wild over their idols. He had weak knees at the sight of his man. He was totally crushing on his boyfriend.

When Reef got up and stepped closer, Ford was already in his personal space, wrapping his arms around him. Reef didn't pause either, hugging him close and burying his face in Ford's neck as his hand came into his hair.

"My cell's flat. I'm sorry if you were worried. I forgot to charge it last night."

"I thought... I have no idea what I thought when you didn't pick up, but yeah, I was freakin' out." Ford pulled back and gazed into Reef's eyes seeing the fear there before letting his own flutter closed and kissing him gently.

Against Reef's lips, he whispered, "I missed you, sweet cheeks."

"Me too, bunnykins."

"Oh God, no." Ford barked out a laugh. "But I do love ya."

"Me too, Ford. I love you, too." A throat being cleared had them both turning toward the sound. "Dad, I'd like to introduce you to my boyfriend, Ford. Ford, you've met Coach before, but he's my dad for all intents and purposes. So, meet my dad."

"Sir," Ford said as he held out his hand for Coach to shake.

"Not Sir, son. You call me Coach or Dad," he replied as he took a hold of Ford's hand and pulled him in for a hug. "I'm so sorry for the way I treated you both. It was unacceptable."

"There's nothing to forgive if you and Reef are okay."

"I think we are. Are we, Reef?"

"Absolutely," Reef nodded, smiling at his pseudo dad.

They sat down and Ford handed over Reef's cookie, smiling as Reef gave him a wicked grin and pushed aside the plate with his half eaten burger to dig into the sweet treat filled with gooey chocolate. The dark liquid oozed out, dripping over his fingers with the first bite and Reef's moan of appreciation had Ford's cock hardening.

"Ford, I think you and Reef should speak about your father. I'll excuse myself so you two can talk."

"No, Dad, it's okay. Stay. We've got no secrets." So he did and as Reef told Ford details of the conversation he'd had with the stranger who called himself Ford's father, the bile rose in his throat. That man was no father to him anymore, not that he'd ever been a stellar example, but still. And his mother's involvement in this plan sickened him even more. They'd tried to divide and conquer them, Ford's father attempting to pay Reef off to make him leave and Ford's mother opening her arms in the hope he'd go to them for comfort. God only knew who they planned on setting him up with on the rebound.

"I feel sick," Ford murmured when he'd heard the whole story. "I knew they were devious but this is beyond anything I've ever imagined." Ford detailed his conversation with his mother to Reef who was speechless too.

"The two of you need a plan. Whatever you resolve to

do make sure you're rock solid. Even a sliver of doubt and they'll capitalize on it to rip you apart," Coach instructed them. "Momma Bear and I are happy to speak with them too. Just let us know when and where to be and we'll take it from there."

"That's a little dangerous." Reef laughed. "I think she'll kick Dr. Wallace's ass if she got her hands on him."

"If it wasn't for you stopping me, *I* would have kicked his ass," Coach replied, shaking his head.

"Maybe we should kick their asses. It'd certainly make me feel better," Ford grumbled. "Jesus, I can't believe they did this."

"I think we should cut off all contact; ignore their calls, emails everything. If they come to see us, we walk away from them, close the door in their faces, whatever." Reef paused when Ford nodded. "But, hon, that's a pretty permanent solution and I'd hate for you to lose them if we hold a grudge, so I'm torn. I wanna say we should give them a chance to fix this and you've told them how, but on the other hand, would they use it against us?" Reef sighed, clearly frustrated. "Maybe we should just tell 'em to go fuck a donkey?"

"I was just about to tell you that you're making me sick with how mature you're being about all this." Ford snorted out a laugh. "I'm glad you're pissed."

"You have no idea, Ford. I'm ready to kill the bastard but I know how much it hurts to lose people you love. I don't wanna give them the chance to spew more poison. I've got better shit to do with my life than listen to that but I don't want you to get hurt either."

Ford grasped Reef's warm hand and brought his knuckles to his lips. Brushing a gentle kiss over them, Ford smiled. "As long as I have you, that's all I need and with

Coach and Momma Bear's support, we have everything we need. How about we let it sit for a while then I'll call them and we can talk to them together. If they're still pulling shit, I'll cut off contact with them."

Reef wrapped his arms around Ford and Ford leaned into the loving touch. Feeling Reef's lips against his temple, he smiled. The weight on his shoulders lifted off. Hope shined on them even though he knew what the reality was — he was giving up his parents, but it was their loss, not his. Cutting ties wasn't the end of the world because as sappy as it sounded, love surrounded him. He didn't need their poor excuse of it. Ford was happy. Uplifted. The grin spread wider; he was smiling like a fool now. Coach met his gaze and the other man smiled too.

"What are you two grinning about?" Reef asked.

"Life's good, sweet. I've got you. Coach is sitting here and you two have worked things out. You're gonna win the world championship this year but even if you don't, you're gonna kick ass. I know you'll be proud of whatever you achieve and... um... never mind." He laughed blushing at the same time, embarrassed to have nearly blurted out he was looking forward to getting Reef naked.

Reef's heated look told him he knew exactly what Ford was thinking. A flame ignited between them as they stared in each other's eyes, drawing them together like an invisible tractor beam until they were breathing each other's air, their lips hovering only a hair's breadth apart.

"That really is my cue to leave," Coach stated, standing up.

"Sorry," Ford mumbled, struggling to think while his cock was hard enough to hammer nails. "Didn't mean to make you feel uncomfortable."

"Son, you didn't make me feel uncomfortable but I

know what love and lust is and you two have it in spades. You should celebrate coming through this together and the last thing you need is an old man being a third wheel. As your Momma would say, cage the snake before you shake 'n' bake."

"Oh, fuck me," Reef moaned, shaking his head. "Could you be any more embarrassing?" Ford couldn't help the snort of laughter from bursting free which only got louder as Reef's face colored in a fierce blush.

"It's my job, and now I get to say it to the two of you, or at least... You know what, never mind. Play it safe."

"We will, Coach," Ford replied, still gasping for breath.

"Dad," Reef said standing up and hugging the older man tight. "Thank you for everything, except embarrassing the hell outta me. I... I don't know what I would have done if I'd lost you."

Pulling back, Coach grasped Reef's biceps in his big hands. "You're my son, Reef. Not by blood but that's never mattered before. You're everything to your Momma and me. Losing you was never an option. I just had to remember that wonderful things can come along when you least expect it. Life didn't give us a child of our own but you've become that. You're everything and more in a son we could ever have asked for."

"I love you, too."

"Always, Reef."

Ford had no words when Coach turned to him and said, "You're my son now too. You'll always be welcome, always have a family and a home with us. No matter what happens with your parents, you're not alone." Ford hoped the tight hug he gave Coach told him how grateful he was for his gift.

As Coach turned and walked away, waving to them as he exited the burger place, Ford looked across to Reef. "I get it now. I get why you idolize the man. He's... wow, he'd have been a great father. You're lucky he was yours growing up."

"Yeah, I am. You're lucky too, you know."

"What, lucky? With my parents? Seriously?" Ford asked, unbelievingly.

"You heard him say it. We're your family too, Ford. You don't need them in your life anymore if they won't support and love you like you deserve. You're a good man, hon, the best. They're the ones missing out if they give you up."

Joining their hands, Ford rested his forehead against his man's. "I love you, Reef. If our life together is gonna be half this good, I can't wait for the rest of it."

Reef paused, pulling back a little to look closely at Ford, almost as if he was assessing him before he hummed and leaned closer again. But the pause was more telling than anything and when Ford pulled back to look at him, Reef asked quietly, "Are you worried about us being apart?"

"Yes and no. I hated not being near you after you left Queenstown; it sucked, big time. It's gonna be hard but am I worried about us getting through it intact? Not at all. I love you, and a little distance isn't gonna change that."

"I love hearing you say that." Reef smiled, but it quickly dropped off his face.

"But you are worried," Ford commented. "What about?"

"The negativity. I don't want it to get to be too much, too hard. I'm scared of losing you because of everyone else's interference." He shrugged his shoulders and looked away, trying to hide from Ford while laying it all on the line; exposing himself completely.

"Sweet cheeks, look at me." Ford cupped Reef's face in both his hands as he gazed into his man's eyes. "I love you. I'll walk away from my parents, from anyone before I let them turn me against you. I'm not gonna hurt you. I'm not gonna leave you. Remember, we're permanent. I'll always wait for you."

Reef blinked, his eyes radiating the warmth that Ford fell so hard for. "Yeah, I remember. You'll hold my spot."

Running his thumb over Reef's bottom lip and pulling his man closer, he brushed a barely-there kiss over Reef's mouth before whispering, "Yeah, Reef. We're rock solid. Everything else is just white noise."

Reef smiled, those sexy as sin dimples showing on each side of his face. Ford knew it deep within. This man was his forever. Whatever the future might hold, they would face it side by side. And life with Reef by his side looked bloody good.

THE END... FOR NOW

WHITEWASH

UNEXPECTED BOOK THREE

Get the continuation of Reef and Ford's story here.

The bus lurched to a stop at the front entry to the resort. Reef took a deep breath and plastered on a fake smile, locking the façade in place as he disembarked the bus and stepped onto the stony surface of the drive. The great timber and stone structure of the four-story building that stretched out along the street towered over him, blocking the view of the ski slope behind it. Grey skies loomed above, the freezing wind cutting through them. Shoulders hunched, he stuffed his hands in his pockets and looked to the luggage being offloaded, wishing he didn't have to deal with the heavy load. His snowboards, boots and ski gear took up the most room, his other stuff crammed into two smaller packs.

"Why don't you leave these, Reef?" Mace squeezed his shoulder again. "I can look after them for you."

"Nah, it's okay." Reef shook his head, dropping his gaze to the gravel underfoot kicking at the small rocks. "It'll give me something to do."

"I'm sorry, man. Totally sucks that he couldn't get the time off."

Reef huffed out a breath and nodded. "Yeah, it does."

"Come on, let's get our shit organized so we can eat. I'm starving." Reef followed Mason's lead, picking up a couple of their bags and joining the line to check-in. As the bus pulled away, the view opened up before him. A heavy covering of snow blanketed the high-pitched roofs of the hotels opposite them, the competition flags blowing in the breeze. Tall pines swayed in the distance, the towering mountain range the resort was nestled in covered in a mist of white as the clouds swirled around their peaks. It would snow that evening. Even since arriving, Reef could sense the shift in the temperature. Leaving Mace in line he wandered over to the arched windows, leaning against the frame as he watched skiers come down off the slopes and dodge the buses and SUVs as they crossed over to their own resorts and the myriad eateries.

Reef toyed with his cell, shooting off a quick message to Ford while he waited.

Skype in 20 mins or tonight, bunnykins? I wanna see you.

People swarmed everywhere around him, bundled up in heavy coats and scarves like bees buzzing around a flower garden. Reef watched them from the sidelines, happy not to be in the fray. He wouldn't be able to stand on the outskirts and watch for much longer though. The event sponsors had set up a signing this time around, rather than the usual meet and greet required with every leg of the tour. Reef could already see the tables being organized in the open ballroom off to the side of the lobby. A bolt of excitement shot through him. Meeting his fans was a hell of a lot of fun. It was exactly what he needed to lift his mood. The little kids were always awesome, always made him grin non-stop. And the fact he even had fans who were loyal enough to stand in line to get something signed or in the freezing cold to watch him still blew him away. Until then, he needed food.

Reef jumped when Mason joined him, leaning against the other window. "You tried calling him yet?"

"Nah, I just messaged him. I think he's got a double shift today."

"Come on, we're checked in. We're sharing a suite again so let's do lunch then you've got the promo sesh."

Reef's tired muscles ached. Lifting his arms above his head he stretched, leaning from side to side. "Do I have time for a quick workout? I'm so damn sore."

"Nope. We arrived late. You're gonna have to suck it up, buttercup. Smile and be your charming self for a while, then you can go for a run."

Reef groaned but cracked a smile when Mace pointed to a guest carrying a hot drink. "Don't worry, I'll keep you caffeinated."

They stepped to the lifts and Reef's cell chimed with an incoming message from Ford.

NSFW.

The picture attachment was exactly that—not safe for work. Ford's hard cock—and it was definitely Ford's cock—took center stage. Rabbit ears, eyes and a grin were drawn on his crown with a bow tie just below it. 'Bunnykins misses you too, sweet cheeks,' was added as a speech bubble. Reef's snort of laughter cut through the quiet of the lift as it slowed to a stop on their floor.

"Whatcha lookin' at?" Mace asked as the lift doors opened and he looked over Reef's shoulder.

"Oh, you don't wanna see." He laughed, darkening the screen. "Trust me." Smirking at Mace, he added, "You really don't wanna see."

His belly uncomfortably full from lunch, Reef slumped in the armchair that was placed in the corner of his room, exhausted. It'd been a grueling few weeks and the non-stop travelling was catching up with him. Closing his eyes, he leaned his head on the backrest and groaned. He needed a workout; not more sitting around.

After a moment, he rummaged around in his bag and pulled out a few shirts. The tee Ford had surprised him with was on top of the pile. Smiling, Reef thought about the morning he'd received the gift.

He cracked open his eyes as the weight between Reef's legs shifted and a warm wet tongue lapped at the crown of his cock. God, had he ever been this hard? Reef moaned, bucking his hips and trying to increase the friction and suction on his throbbing shaft.

"Morning, sleepyhead."

"Suck me, Ford. Please," he gasped as Ford wrapped his hand around the base of Reef's dick and pumped him languidly. Ford knew every hot button to press and Reef erupted in record time to Ford fingering his ass and his tongue sneaking out to lap at his balls each time Ford deep-throated him. How he did that while using enough suction to rival a Hoover, Reef would never know.

When the world stopped spinning and Reef had caught his breath, he rolled Ford off him, caging him below his body.

Grinding against his man's erection, Reef's spent dick perked up at the possibility of a second orgasm. "Gonna keep you in bed all day, Ford. You're gonna fuck me over and over until I can't walk straight. Wanna feel you for days."

"Oh God, yes," Ford moaned, gripping Reef's hips to press him down, sliding his cock against him. "Shit, wait," Ford grumbled. "Need to...." he trailed off, shifting on the sheets.

Reef pinched Ford's nipple and rocked his hips, murmuring against his throat. "Only thing we need is lube, hon. Gotta have you inside me."

Ford shifted again and Reef sat up giving him some room. Arching his back, Ford pulled a wrapped package from beneath him, squashed when Reef rolled them over. Tossing it aside, Ford reached up to pull Reef's face down to his again but Reef was intrigued. "What is it, hon?"

"No big deal. I'll show you later."

"Nah, I wanna see what you got me." Reef said playfully, reaching across the bed for the package now haphazardly balancing on the edge of the mattress. Tearing open the bright blue tissue paper, two bundles of material fell out. White T-shirts with black sleeves. On one was written He sucks *and on the other* I swallow. *Surprised, Reef turned to Ford who met his gaze with a sheepish smile and a shrug.*

"Aww, how romantic, bunnykins. You got me a shirt to wear next time we meet your Mom and Dad," Reef teased.

Ford laughed. "God, I'd pay to see that."

"You know, you might even get lucky later giving me gifts like this." Reef wiggled his eyebrows.

Laughing again, Ford replied, "That was the idea, sweet cheeks."

Reef's cell, beeping a message alarm, startled him back to reality. The words on the screen had him digging through his bags to find his tablet and loading up Skype so he could video-chat with his man. Ford would be on in ten minutes. Ten minutes and he'd be able to see him again. Grinning, Reef brought up the app. Ford was already online. He gave a sigh of relief and dialed. The familiar ringtone barely sounded before his call was answered. But the sight greeting him surprised Reef. A woman—Gabriella—stood before him smiling at the screen. Long dark brown hair and matching brown eyes, flawless olive skin and a face too pretty for anything other than a magazine cover had Reef swallowing. She was beautiful. No stunning. Stunningly beautiful.

"*Ciao*," she said happily in a strong Italian accent. "I'm Gabriella, Ford's friend."

Reef smiled. "Hi, I'm Reef."

"I know. Ford speaks of you all the time. *Un momento*, he's here. *Arrivederci!*" The vision onscreen blurred, as if the camera was being moved far too fast to focus and Ford's smiling face appeared.

"God, it's good to see you, Reef. I've missed you."

"I'm lucky, I got to see a whole lot more of you this morning." Reef grinned wickedly at Ford's blush.

"Too much?"

Reef laughed. "Mace almost copped an eyeful but I'm always glad to see any part of you. If we're naming our junk though, I want something manly, like Chuck Norris."

"Yeah, okay. I'll go MacGyver then. Or Indiana Jones."

Reef clicked his fingers and pointed. "I've got it. Donkey dick."

Ford laughed. "Stallion could work. I could buck you all night long." Reef coughed out another laugh.

Putting on a fake drawl and tipping an imaginary hat, Reef responded, "I'll ride you like a Texan cowboy."

Ford's fingertips brushed the screen, giving Reef a warm smile. "I love hearing you laugh," Ford murmured and Reef's smile turned shy. They didn't have long—Reef had to be at the signing in a few, but there was no way he wasn't making use of every short-lived moment together. His heart fluttered every time Ford smiled at him. With every word of encouragement Ford uttered, Reef fell harder. It was so damn hard being apart from him. His heart ached from the distance between them, but these stolen moments meant everything. They were literally what kept Reef going. Knowing Ford was missing him just as much gave Reef some sort of perverse comfort—he didn't want Ford in pain, but knowing he wasn't the only one of them who was lonely was reassuring. And times like these, where they had a chance just to tease each other and get back to that levity they always had, lifted Reef's spirits. So, while he would do almost anything to have those strong arms wrapped around him tight— including playing hooky with the competition—Reef tried to use the desire as motivation. You know, for good instead of evil. But hell, it'd be good times to get Ford alone for a few hours again.

Reef's cock twitched thinking of all the despicable things they could do to each other. By the heated expression Ford gave him— all intense eyes and a slow wetting of his bottom lip with the tongue that could take Reef to heaven and back— he had clued into Reef's inner monologue. Reef stole a look at his watch. *Fuck it.* He didn't want to be a Debbie Downer, but he was way too short on time to do anything. And there was no way Reef could do a signing with a raging boner. He groaned and scrubbed his forehead in frustration. Thankfully, Ford took the hint and steered their conversation back into safer territory, telling Reef how

Gabriella and Alfonso, the bar tender at their local looked like they might finally make the move from friends to lovers.

"Shit, hon, I've got to go or I'm gonna be late. I'm sorry, I've got to get downstairs for this signing."

"Don't be, sweet. I'll take five minutes over nothing any day. I love you."

"Love you too, Ford. I miss you."

"Me too." Ford touched his fingertips to the screen and Reef followed suit, joining them in the only connection they could have in that moment. Hundreds, hell possibly even thousands of miles of road separated them but for that instant, Reef was back in his arms in Queenstown dancing, or hugging him from behind as Ford stirred up a mean casserole on the stove in their townhouse in Fernie.

A LIL' BONUS

A LIL' BONUS – COFFEE WITH REEF AND FORD

A gust of icy wind blasted us as Ford held the door open for me to step through, before he and Reef entered. I shook the snow off my coat and wiped the mud from my boots as the boys did the same. Looking around the lodge's coffee shop, I could see why Reef loved it so much. It was warm and friendly—much like the rest of Fernie—and the smell of sweet cinnamon and vanilla, hazelnut, and freshly ground coffee tempted me to breathe deep. The manager had sectioned off an area for us, happy to host a private party for one of their favorite patrons and his boyfriend. We made our way over to the gathering of tables in the corner of the room and I couldn't help but get excited at the prospect of meeting so many friends who I'd spoken to for so long online. Meeting them face-to-face was pretty freaking cool.

Inhaling the addictive smells, I dropped my bag over the thick rope onto one of the three spare seats at the long table, before looking around at the gathering of friends already seated. I saw Ford smirk at me. Mirroring his smile, I moved to the opening in the rope barrier and greeted a few familiar faces. Ford's laugh had me looking up at both he and Reef. Furrowing my brows in confusion, their laughter made sense when, still holding hands, they lifted their long legs and gracefully stepped over the rope. I mock-scowled at them, barely concealing my grin, as I placed my laptop on the table.

Ann:Not all of us can be tall and gorgeous, thank you Reef and Ford, (*I muttered under my breath. Turning my attention to all the ladies gathered around them, I spoke up, projecting my voice to the group.*) Thanks everyone for joining us here at Fernie Lodge. This is Reef's favorite coffee shop, so you know the cakes and cookies are gonna be good. A bit of housekeeping first —there's no need to go to the counter for your orders; we've got table service today so order whatever you'd like. Once we're all comfortable, we can get started.

Seeing a few nods around the group, I turned to Reef and Ford who smiled and nodded at me.

Okay then, I'd like to introduce you all to Reef Reid and Ford Wallace. Anyone who'd like to ask the boys a question, fire away.

Reef and Ford waved to the fans already seated at the tables, taking up most of the coffee shop. Snagging the two chairs saved for them, Ford took off his coat and placed it in Reef's outstretched arms, before sitting down. I followed, pulling my computer onto my lap.

Ford:Wow, what an amazing turnout. Hi ladies, lads.

Reef: Thanks for coming. (*Reef looked around the room, grinning.*) I had no idea how many of you Ann invited. She told us it was gonna be coffee with a few friends; this is a party. Awesome.

Ford:So anyone wanna go first?

Casey Krees:I will. (*She raised her hand and waved to get their attention, blushing when Ford grinned at her.*) What's your funniest moment together?

Ford:Umm... (*Ford looked thoughtful for a moment, furrowing his brow.*) There's so many of them. Lemmie come back to that one. I've gotta think up something that'll embarrass Reef.

Reef:(*Reef nudged him in the ribs, shaking his head.*) You aren't without embarrassing moments either, bunnykins. I'm not the only dork in this relationship.

The warmth from the nearby fireplace had me cooking in all my cold-weather gear. I stripped off my heavy coat, scarf, beanie and gloves I was still wearing and pushed up my sleeves.

Ann:God, we should have chosen a warmer climate for this coffee. At least they have the heat cranked up to inferno levels. Tell me again why we chose a mountain lodge?

Reef:Hey, you told us 'I'll come to you. Everyone's keen to see you in action before the season. I love the snow,' so stop whining. We'll come and stay on the Gold Coast after the season's over, okay wuss?

Ann:You know I can write you into some really awkward moments, Reef? Do you seriously wanna risk that?

I arched my eyebrow at Reef and he responded with a wicked grin. Chuckling, Ford threw his arm around my shoulders.

Ford: Shortie, bring it on. Hit us with your best shot.

I threw up my hands in mock-frustration as Ford and most of our friends who had joined us laughed at me.

Ann:(*I put on my best 'mom' voice and pointed a finger*

at both of them.) Wait until Whitewash. You guys are gonna regret being smart asses with me.

Loving the lighthearted banter, I couldn't help but laugh when Ford shook his head, still grinning at me.

Ford:Bring it.

Casey Krees:Can I ask another question? (*Reef nodded at her and she smiled back at him.*) Would you ever let a girl into the mix for a one-nighter?

Reef's wide-eyed stare was comical, almost as much as the shade of red Ford turned giving away his jealousy. And I couldn't help thinking Payback's a bitch, baby! while laughing at their reactions.

Ann:I told you guys that nothing was off limits. Cough up the answer.

Reef:Um, I'd say yes if Ford really wanted to but she has to know I'm not giving him up for her, so she's strictly a one-nighter.

Ford:(*Ford looked aghast at Reef.*) Oh hell no! No-one is getting their hands on you, guy or girl.

Casey Krees:Aww. Well it would have been totally hot.

Casey giggled and Reef snorts out a laugh shaking his head at Ford. As Ford visibly tried to calm down and wrestle the not-so-little green eyed monster of his into submission, I watched as Reef squeezed his hand capturing Ford's gaze. Ford's description was on the money – Reef's eyes were really the warmest of browns and they danced with love.

Reef:Just you and me, okay? (*Ford took a deep breath and nodded, looking calmer with Reef's words.*) Always, just you and me.

Ford:Yeah, just us.

Leaning forward and dropping a sweet kiss on Ford's lips, Reef turned to the room and smiled.

Reef: Good to know we started with the easy questions. Who's next?

Jamie Nibarger Ellis:I've got a question too. Who's bigger ... down there?

Reef:Me.

Ford:Me.

In unison:Him.

Jamie Nibarger Ellis:So modest.

Reef:Actually, Ford is thicker and I'm longer.

Ford:Aww, honey buns, you make me hot when you're sweet. (*Ford murmured quietly to his man, before grasping his face and crushing their mouths together.*)

A chorus of sighs sounded from around the room, but by the looks of how wrapped up in each other Ford and Reef were, their audience could have been a million miles away. The chemistry between the two of them was obvious to everyone in the room.

Joelle Mendes:You're killing me here. I'm gonna need to attack my husband soon.

Pulling back, Ford breathed hard, still staring at Reef before turning to Joelle. I could see how much he struggled to hide the arousal, but the rasp in his voice gave him away just how hot and hard he was. Well, that and the massive tent which had formed in his jeans.

Ford:We're glad to be of service.

Joelle laughed and fanned herself, breaking the sexual tension in the room.

Dawn Nicole Costiera:So, what's your type?

Reef:Ford.

Reef cleared his throat, shifting in the seat and spreading his legs, giving the boner, I could see, a little more room.

Reef:But if we're talking girls, I've always gone for

supermodel looks. Shame there hasn't been any substance behind those looks in the ones I've dated.

Ford leaned back in the armchair and looked thoughtful for a moment, playing with the material of Reef's thermal shirt. Reef's shiver was subtle when Ford's fingertips brushed his back.

Ford:Um, I don't think I really have a type in girls. You might think I've been kind of a slut, but it's not that. I like sex. I love it and I loved being with women in the past. It didn't matter what they looked like, it was always their personality that grabbed me —feistiness, being high on life, funny, happy, smart, quiet. If I felt an attraction, I went with it. But it's completely different with Reef; he's the whole package. There's a physical pull between us which is crazy—I literally can't keep my hands off him—but he's also become my best friend in such a short time. We clicked, every element fell into place and I've never been happier. So, while in the past it was certain aspects of a person, with Reef it's everything. He's it for me, definitely.

Reef smiled at Ford, the love radiating from their connection made me sigh. From my position next to them, I could see Reef slide his hand under the table and squeeze Ford's leg, resting his palm on his thigh. Within a second, Ford was grinning like a love-struck teenager.

Casey Krees:Who's the more dominant one?

Reef:Ford. He's a protector and I love that.

Barely the sliver of distance between them seemed to be too much for the men because Ford wrapped his arms around Reef again and leaned their heads together, snuggling into him.

Dawn Nicole Costiera:Hard or soft? Wine, beer, or liquor? Party hard or just chill?

Ford:Hard or soft – either one can be just as good, but

we tend to come together pretty hard for round one, then round two is a lot slower and softer. Beer or whiskey. Not a wine fan, mainly because it pisses my parents off that I don't drink it with all the sophisticated people. And what was the third question? Partying? As long as Reef's with me, it doesn't matter what we do.

Reef:Aww, bunnykins, you're so damn romantic. (*Reef batted his eyes at Ford, smiling sweetly at him as the room erupted in laughter at the pet name — myself included*).

Ford rubbed his forehead with his free hand and cursed under his breath as an embarrassed blush crept up his neck.

Ford:Fuck, that name's awful Reef. How do I get you to stop using it? Name a sexual favor. Seriously, anything.

Reef's grin turned wicked and he looked to Ford's lap as he inched his hand closer to Ford's package. Ford's eyes widened in shock as Reef's hand closed over his now straining cock, giving it a squeeze before he pulled away. I had to cover my mouth to stop the laughter bubbling up. Ford was dumbstruck but the need coursing through him was evident from the fire in his eyes. I've never seen such a heated glance pass between two people. It was damn near inferno levels.

Reef:So... (*Reef cleared his throat and shivered when Ford leaned in and sucked on the soft skin below his ear.*) Next question?

Natalie Weston:Describe each other in one word.

Ford:Cheesy usually, but today he's the devil.

Ford adjusted himself as casually as possible. But I was pretty sure that with every eye in the room on him, their gaze were drawn down in the direction of his moving hand. I know mine was.

Ford:Actually, no he's pretty bloody amazingly talented and ballsy for taking the jumps he does. I'm in awe when I watch him on the slopes. (*Reef cuddled into Ford.*)

Reef:I'd go with ... heroic. Not superhero in Lycra heroic, but he saves lives. Literally. And he's a good man, you know? He'd take the shirt off his back if you needed it. I'm the one in awe; I'm so lucky to have met him. He says I'm brave, but I just take a jump off a mountain. What I do is nothing compared to what Ford does.

Natalie Weston:I can really feel the love you guys have for each other.

Reef:Yeah, he's my boo. (*Ford smirked at Reef.*)

Ford:You're a nutter.

Joelle Mendes:What quality of your partner makes you sure they'd be an awesome father?

Reef:He's that guy you look up to. (*Reef held up his hand to stop the giggles.*) I know, I'm a sap. He's just... I dunno. If I'm being really corny—and hell, you're already laughing at me—I'd say he gives great hugs.

Joelle Mendes:Aww.

Ford:Hon, c'mere. (*Ford pulled Reef even closer before pressing a kiss to his cheek.*) Reef's a big kid, but in the best possible way. He'll be a great dad because he'd relate to kids so well and he has so much love to give.

Ford kissed Reef again, a lingering sweet kiss that had me smiling. They're so cute together.

Joelle Mendes:Damn.

Ford: You'll be an amazing dad, hon. I can't wait to see you with kids. (*Reef leaned his head on Ford's shoulder.*)

Reef: Hit us with your next question, or I'm whisking him away.

Nicole Dawn Costiera:Beach or city?

Ford:I'd say beach. Growing up in London was enough to make me want open spaces. That's one of the reasons why I jumped at the opportunity of working on the slopes. Normally at this time of year I'm in the South of France but I obviously skipped it for Canada this year. You've read about some of the other reasons why and all about our 'adventures' (*Ford held up and curled his index and middle fingers over, mimicking quotation marks with his hands.*)—here in Canada in White Noise.

Reef: (*Reef snorted out a laugh, lacking in any humor.*) Yeah, adventures. I don't think I've ever been as stressed in my life. And yeah, I'm gonna need a beach soon too. Any suggestions on sunblock? I'm gonna burn like a crisp.

Ann:I've got some of the good stuff at home. You can use it.

Mari Cárdenas:What's your favorite song?

Ford:There's one by Darren Hayes that always gets me. It's called *'Taken by the Sea'*. Michelle Booklover Simm put me onto it. I'd heard it a few times before, but when I hit rock bottom, it played on the radio. It made me realize how much I have. Love it. Great song.

Reef:For me it's Charlie Puth's *'One Call Away.'* Reminds me of that night in Queenstown at the sports bar. You remember it, hon?

Ford:Yeah, I remember everything about that night. (*Ford nodded, smiling at Reef.*)

That was one of my favorite parts of their story together. Making that commitment to each other to stay together after Reef's holiday in New Zealand had ended always made me smile.

Mari Cárdenas:I love Darren Hayes, Ford. I'll have to find that one. Haven't heard anything by Charlie Puth, but I'll remedy that soon. (*Mari smiled at the guys and typed something on her cell.*)

Reef:It's the Superman song, the one out of Fast 7.

You'll know it as soon as you hear it, Mari. I love anything Blink 182, Powderfinger, Chili Peppers, Metallica – all the classics too. Good tunes to rock out to on the snow.

Ford:Yeah, great songs, and Powderfinger was so good live. Best concert I've seen.

Niki Sass:So who's your celeb crush?

Reef:Ford, hon, I'm answering this one for you. (*Reef patted Ford's knee and smirked at him.*)

Ford:Oh, geez, here we go. (*Ford rolled his eyes. Reef grinned wickedly at him.*)

I could see why Ford was hooked on Reef's dimples. Damn, the man was sexy when he flashed them. Seriously swoon-worthy.

Reef:Me. No lie. It's me. Can you believe it? He actually followed my career for years before we met and didn't even recognize me. Un-freaking-believable. (*Reef shook his head and playfully elbowed Ford in the ribs.*)

Ford:Yeah, busted. I know, shameful. Reef's is Caden Lambert, the current world champion.

Niki Sass:Thank you, you're both too adorable.

Reef glared at Ford, but I could tell it was fake.

Reef:You're a shit, Ford. You know that? You all got to know a little about Caden in White Noise. He's a pain in my ass and so *not* my celeb crush. That'd have to be Charlize Theron; she's my hall pass.

I smirked and a few people laughed.

Niki Sass:Ford, you should be mad at that. You'll get to have make-up sex.

Ford:Who's mad? I'd get to watch.

Reef:Yeah, right. That'll be the day. You said no to a three-some before.

This time more people broke into giggles at Reef's put-on pout.

Niki Sass:You could pretend to be mad.

Ford:(*Ford growled.*) Angry enough? I'm up for make-up sex anytime. Should we go?

Ford motioned to the door, half standing as he laughed at me shaking my head exasperatedly at him.

Niki Sass:Can I watch? I won't make a sound. (*Ford barked out a laugh as Niki made a zipping motion with her thumb and index finger along the seam of her lips.*) It's purely for research purposes.

The last had Reef laughing too and motioning to himself.

Reef:You couldn't handle watching all of *this* in action.

Jennifer Hoyle:So, what's your number one fear?

Ford's smile dampened and he sat back down. It was as if he wind had been knocked out of his sails. Knowing Ford, knowing how much responsibility he placed on himself for others, it had to be hard on him. Taking a deep breath before he spoke, he blurted out the words.

Ford:Failing. Not in an arrogant way, but failing my patients.

Reef took a hold of Ford's hand and brushed his lips across Ford's knuckles, kissing them. He may have a celeb crush on Charlize Theron, but Ford was clearly Reef's hero.

Reef:You're their savior, Ford. You'd never fail them. (*Turning to the group, Reef continued.*) My number one fear is snakes. Hate the bastards. That's why I live in the snow. Those suckers don't come anywhere near me.

Ford's smile showed just how grateful to Reef he was for redirecting the focus off himself.

Ford:You're safe anywhere in New Zealand. No snakes there.

Reef:Done. If there was any doubt about where I wanted to be, there isn't now. I'm moving to New Zealand.

Jennifer Hoyle:What's your sexual fantasy?

Reef:(*Reef blushed.*) Um, Charlize Theron and Ford?

Ford: (*Ford laughed.*) No girls! I'm thinking Reef splayed out in front of me and I get to do anything I want to him.

Reef:You do that every night.

Ford:Sue me, I'm being sweet. (*Ford shrugged, the blush staining his cheeks belying his embarrassment.*)

JJ Harper:Can I watch?

Reef:I thought our lives were already an open book?

Joelle Mendes:(*Joelle put her hand up and waved it around.*) I wanna watch too.

JJ Harper:(*JJ laughed, nodding.*) That's very true, Reef.

Ford:Yeah, you've already seen some. But there's definitely more to come, and I'm told I'm pretty flexible. There was that shit-hot scene in White Noise.

Ford looked at Reef, the heat between them igniting like dry kindling in a forest fire.

Ford:We'll have to try that again, sweet.

I didn't hear Reef's moan so much as saw Ford's response to it— the full body shiver that wracked him was hot.

Tammie:Reef, would you give up your career to be with Ford?

Reef:In a heartbeat, without one second's hesitation—

Ford:Hell no you wouldn't. You—

Reef:(*Reef held up his hand to halt Ford's interruption.*) I would give up my career without a second's hesitation to be with Ford, *but* he'd never ask me to do it. He'd bust his ass so that I wouldn't have to; but for him, I would.

Ann:You haven't answered Casey's question yet – what's your funniest moment together?

Ford:We've had so many great laughs, it's hard to narrow it down. I think one of the funniest was during the game of twenty questions we played a few nights into Reef staying with me in Queenstown. It was a laugh when we did it in the ranger's cabin, so after we'd seen each other naked, we figured we could ask anything. I asked him to admit what he'd thought about that first night we'd stayed in the cabin when he went to sleep. He admitted that he'd fantasized about me.

Ford gave Casey a self-satisfied smirk that turned into a wicked grin. I could only imagine what was going through his head at that moment.

Reef:He jacked off to thoughts of me, too. Great minds and all that. (*Reef shrugged and smiled shyly.*) It was pretty fucking funny watching Ford get all flustered at admitting it out loud.

Casey Krees: Damn, sweet, and hot much?

Ford:Karaoke.

Reef:(*Reef snorted out a laugh.*) Hell yeah, karaoke was a riot. (*Turning to the rest of the tables gathered around them, Reef grinned.*) Picture this: Ford stands up and half drunk off his ass stumbles over to the mic. When the music starts, he sings every word of Cindi Lauper's '*Girls Just Wanna Have Fun*'. It was like cats screeching, but we cheered him on like a rock star. By the end of it, he thought he was shit-hot and decided to dance too. Yeah, not good.

Ford:Hey, all I have to say is Backstreet Boys.

Reef:I was good. Unlike you, I sang it. I didn't wail it.

Ford:You think you did. I was impressed by how well you knew the dance moves.

Ford stood and shimmied his ass, obviously mimicking Reef's actions as he did a few hand moves and sung 'Everybody (Backstreet's Back Alright)', finishing in a 'Stayin' Alive' pose. And yeah, the singing was out of tune.

Ford: You never struck me as a closeted Backstreet Boys fan.

Reef:I'm not. But it's my karaoke song.

Reef didn't pull off the innocent look well and couldn't hide the blush which crept up his face when we all kept staring at him.

Reef: Oh, okay, alright. I learnt the moves when I was a kid. My friend's older sister was hung-up on them and I liked her, so I learned the dance.

Ford's chuckle turned into a full laugh and with a hand on his abs, he doubled over, no doubt imagining Reef practicing.

Ford dashed the tears from his eyes and laughed harder when he looked at Reef again. Finally calming down, he wiped his face again and shook his head.

Ford: You didn't just admit that did you? You crack me up, sweet.

Reef:Shut up. (*He pouted and Ford wrapped his arms around Reef again and pulled him close, still grinning.*)

Ford: Sweet cheeks, don't ever change. I love the closeted Backstreet Boys fan that you are.

Reef:You're pushing your luck, bunnykins. You know that, don't you? (*Reef laughed and leaned in to press his lips against Ford's.*)

Wrapped up in each other, Ford nuzzled Reef's throat. Ford's whisper barely reached my ears— and that was only because I leaned in to eavesdrop.

Ford:I love you, Reef. Don't ever change.

Ann:I think that's all we have time for, everybody. We're heading up onto the slopes in a few minutes to watch Reef do a couple of runs for us. You're all welcome to join us. Thank you for coming today. Hope you've enjoyed the chance to get to know Reef and Ford a little better.

Reef:Before we go, my sponsors have given me some gear to sign and give out. Stick around for that, too.

Reef pointed to the gym bag full of goodies Mason had carried into the coffee shop earlier that morning.

Reef: Thanks for coming. It's been fun.

Ford:Ladies, lads, it's been a pleasure. Thanks for having us.

Ford smiled and waved to everyone as he stood and moved over to pick up the big bag and drop it at Reef's feet as I moved over to shepherd my friends into a line.

A note from Ann:

When I hit publish on Whiteout, I was crazy nervous. It was my first novel-length MM story released into the big wide world. I'm so humbled by the overwhelmingly positive response I received and by how much love you've shown Reef and Ford. Thank you for all that love. This isn't the end of their story! Check out Whitewash now (and you'll be happy to know that the boys also make an appearance in Delectable).

By day Ann Grech lives in the corporate world and can be found sitting behind a desk typing away at reports and papers or lecturing to a room full of students. She graduated with a PhD in 2016 and is now an over-qualified nerd. Glasses, briefcase, high heels and a pencil skirt, she's got the librarian look nailed too. If only they knew! She swears like a sailor, so that's got to be a hint. The other one was "the look" from her tattoo artist when she told him that she wanted her kids initials "B" and "J" tattooed on her foot. It took a second to register that it might be a bad idea.

She's never entirely fit in and loves escaping into a book —whether it's reading or writing one. But she's found her tribe now and loves her MM book world family. She dislikes cooking, but loves eating, can't figure out technology, but is addicted to it, and her guilty pleasure is Byron Bay Cookies. Oh and shoes. And lingerie. And maybe handbags too. Well, if we're being honest, we'd probably have to add her library too given the state of her credit card every month (what can she say, she's a bookworm at heart)!

She also publishes her raunchier short stories under her pen name, Olive Hiscock.

Ann loves chatting to people online, so if you'd like to keep up with what she's got going on:

Join her newsletter:

http://anngrech.us8.list-manage2.com/subscribe?
u=0af7475c0791ed8f1466e7fd9&id=1cee9cdcb6
Like her on Facebook:
https://www.facebook.com/pages/Ann-
Grech/458420227655212
Join her reader group:
https://www.facebook.com/groups/1871698189780535/
Follow her on Twitter:
@anngrechauthor
Follow her on Goodreads:
https://www.goodreads.com/author/show/7536397.Ann_
Grech
Follow her on BookBub:
https://www.bookbub.com/authors/ann-grech
Follow her on Instagram: @anngrechauthor
Visit her website for her current booklist:
www.anngrech.com

She'd love to hear from you directly, too. Please feel free to
e-mail her at ann@anngrech.com or check out her website
www.anngrech.com for updates.

 instagram.com/anngrechauthor